WI

ANNE
STUART

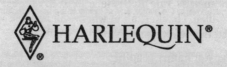

HARLEQUIN®

TORONTO • NEW YORK • LONDON
AMSTERDAM • PARIS • SYDNEY • HAMBURG
STOCKHOLM • ATHENS • TOKYO • MILAN • MADRID
PRAGUE • WARSAW • BUDAPEST • AUCKLAND

ISBN 0-373-16845-4

WILD THING

Visit us at www.eHarlequin.com

Printed in U.S.A.

He was beautiful.

The pictures had been astonishing enough, but they failed to prepare her for the reality of the wild man....

There was no other word for him. Beneath the tangle of long dark hair, beneath the deeply tanned skin and rough beard, he was absolutely stunning. Libby let her eyes run down the entire length of his body, his lean, muscled shoulders and chest, his long legs ending in bare, narrow feet.

She stared at him in awe and fascination, silent, wondering. Most definitely masculine, most definitely human, most definitely him.

It was her worst failing as a scientist. She couldn't disassociate from her subject. But it was hard to be objective when the subject under her examination was a living, breathing, potent male.

Dear Reader,

Have we got a month of great reading for you! Four very different stories by four talented authors—with, of course, all of the romantic exhilaration you've come to expect from a Harlequin American Romance.

National bestselling author Anne Stuart is back and her fabulous book, *Wild Thing*, will get your heart racing. This is a hero you won't soon forget. This month also continues our HAPPILY WEDDED AFTER promotion with *Special Order Groom*, a delightful reunion story by reader favorite, Tina Leonard.

And let us welcome two new authors to the Harlequin American Romance family. Leanna Wilson, a Harlequin Temptation and Silhouette Romance author, brings us a tender surprise pregnancy book with *Open in Nine Months*. And brand-new author Michele Dunaway makes her sparkling debut with *A Little Office Romance*—get ready to have this bachelor boss hero steal your heart.

Next month we have a whole new look in store for our readers—you'll notice our new covers as well as fantastic promotions such as RETURN TO TYLER and brand-new installments in Muriel Jensen's WHO'S THE DADDY? series. Watch for your favorite authors such as Jule McBride, Judy Christenberry and Cathy Gillen Thacker, all of whom will be back with new books in the coming months.

Wishing you happy reading,

Melissa Jeglinski
Associate Senior Editor
Harlequin American Romance

ABOUT THE AUTHOR

Anne Stuart was first published at age 7 in *Jack and Jill* magazine. She wrote her first novel in 1974 and has since published in a variety of genres, including gothics, regencies, suspense and contemporary romance. She particularly likes the spice and danger mixed with the emotional turmoil of romance. She currently lives in the mountains of Vermont with her husband and two children.

Books by Anne Stuart

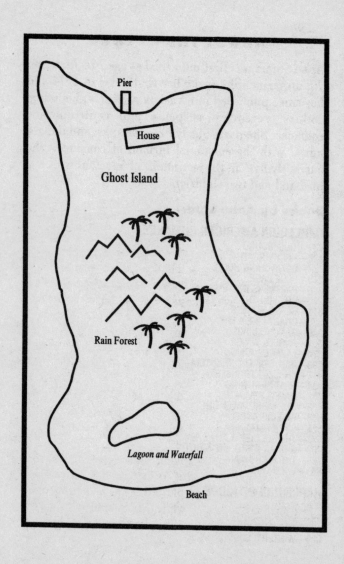

Prologue

It was bloody hell being a minion, Alf Droggan thought grumpily. It was a far cry from what he'd planned, growing up in the mean streets of London. He could have been a bookie like dear old Da. Or a pub owner, or even a judge, if he'd ever bothered to pay attention to Latin during his years at Saint Mary's School of the Innocents. Not that there'd been anyone innocent in that place, from the nuns to the scrubby young malcontents who'd filled the seats and did their time.

That was where he'd met Mick Brown. They made a good pair, the two of them. Mick was small, wiry, ferret-faced and quick. People assumed he was the smart, mean one.

Alf was big, slow-moving, slow-speaking, seemingly a simple soul. But in fact he had twice the brains poor Mick was blessed with, and he could be mean as a snake, while Mick tended to take things as they came.

They'd been together for more than thirty years now, mates since they'd been in the detention center together, and no one, not bosses, not cops, not the occasional wife or girlfriend, got in the way of their bond.

And in fact, they'd landed in the gravy this time. Security consultants to Edward J. Hunnicutt himself. Ed Hunnicutt, the seventh-richest man in the world, working fast on becoming number one. Security consultants, when Hunnicutt had security companies at his beck and call. It was just another term for minion.

But a well-paid minion for all that, Alf thought, leaning back in his leather chair and reaching in his pocket for his ciggies. They weren't there, of course. Old Ed was a health fanatic, and there was no smoking anywhere near him. Couldn't be a proper minion without a cigarette, Alf thought grumpily.

Mick was sitting by the two-way mirror, his nose pressed up against the glass, endlessly fascinated by what lay beyond it. Hell, he might just as well be sitting with his face up against a mirror—Mick was easily amused.

"Alf," Mick said excitedly. "He's starting to move. Can I hit him with the stuff again?"

"Not yet, Mick," Alf said. "Last time we gave him too much and he started twitching. What do you think Old Ed would do if we accidentally killed the bugger?''

"Yeah, but if we wait he might wake up enough to do some damage. He's right huge, he is.''

"Then we'll do like we did last time. One of us takes the hypodermic, the other covers him with the tranquilizer gun. He's not breaking any more of my bones. He tries it again, I'll break his neck,'' Alf said, shifting his cast. At least it was his right arm, and he was left-handed. He'd still managed to fight the bastard off and jam the needle into his arm so hard it had broken. And then when he'd dropped to the floor Alf had satisfied himself by kicking him in the face.

Old Ed hadn't been pleased by the mess he'd made of his prize possession. He'd spoken quite sharply, and Alf had had to apologize. Minion or not, Alf knew that Ed Hunnicutt was richer than the queen, and he paid well for brute force and discretion. Things that Alf and Mick specialized in.

He wasn't finished with the thing locked behind the thick, mirrored glass. He didn't dare touch him again until Old Ed lost interest, but his time would come. No one messed with Alf Droggan and got away with a few a bruises. He'd get what was his.

"He's waking up,'' Mick said, his voice high-pitched with excitement. "Come on, Alf. Let me get the needle. I won't give him too much, I promise.''

"All right, Mick," Alf said kindly. "You go ahead. The lady's coming soon, and we don't want her to be scared away by him. Not that Old Ed's money won't overcome any scruples she might have."

"Money can't buy everything, Alf," Mick said, cheerfully heading for the drug cabinet.

"Can't prove that by me. Or by anyone I've ever met," Alf said. "They all have their price. Old Ed will get the lady doctor jumping when he snaps his fingers, just like we do." Another minion, he thought. Just what Edward J. Hunnicutt needed.

Chapter One

Dr. Elizabeth Holden had never been so tired in her entire life. It didn't make sense—she'd spent the last eighteen hours comfortably ensconced in a first-class airplane seat, with every amenity she could possibly want. She'd dutifully taken walks every hour to stretch her muscles, she'd slept deeply and well, and since she'd deliberately removed her watch the time changes shouldn't be affecting her.

Of course, the last jog in that tiny deathtrap of a plane could be the reason. She hated small planes with a coward's passion. She wasn't overly enthusiastic about the big ones, either, but at least she felt marginally safer in them. She'd almost refused to get onto the small plane waiting to take her to Ghost Island, and in the end it was only her precarious self-respect that made her do it.

She'd survived the flight, but just barely, and she was ready to get on with her task.

She hated not having her watch, just hated it. She needed order and regulation in her life, and not wearing her watch made her feel vulnerable. A small price to pay, but she hated it.

She leaned back against the leather seat of the limo, wondering if she could search through her briefcase and put her watch back on, now that her journey was almost at an end. But then she'd have to ask the huge, monosyllabic driver what time it was in this time zone, and she wasn't sure she really wanted to know.

She glanced out the window at the tropical growth. It was early evening, she guessed, though for all she knew it could be just after dawn. Shadows lurked beneath the lush forest that surrounded the narrow road, and she wondered just what kind of wildlife lay hidden back there.

Not snakes, she hoped. Libby hated snakes with a simple, terrifying passion. But this was an island, a huge private island off in the middle of nowhere. Weren't islands free of snakes? Ireland was, if Saint Patrick had done his job properly, and so was Hawaii. She could only trust this remote island was similarly snake-free.

She sighed, shoving a hand through her short-cropped hair. It must be nice to be the seventh-richest man in the world, she thought. Edward J. Hunnicutt could have absolutely anything he wanted, be it a large private island somewhere in the general area of Australia, be it an entire university at his bidding, be it an up-and-coming research anthropologist who hated snakes and didn't like to leave civilization.

When Edward J. Hunnicutt snapped his fingers, the president of Stansfield University jumped, and the entire faculty followed. It was Hunnicutt who supported the entire science department, Hunnicutt who funded Libby's research and position. Hunnicutt who wanted Libby to drop everything, get on a plane and fly halfway across the world to conduct research on his newest finding.

And Libby jumped, dropped and flew as ordered. Grant money was the name of the game in research, and Hunnicutt was a billionaire with a hobby and agenda. He wasn't content with earning a fortune so staggering that Libby couldn't even begin to imagine it. He wanted to be responsible for great scientific achievements, and he was willing to buy them, no matter what the price.

And obviously Libby Holden was willing to be bought. The thought should have depressed her, but at the moment she was simply grateful someone wanted her.

Don't think about it, she ordered herself. *So Richard decided he'd rather sleep with graduate students than marry you. Fine and dandy.* Sex was overrated, Richard was a pompous bore, and she'd do much better concentrating on her career than a failed relationship that had been over for more than a year.

But the fact of the matter was, Richard had expected to be Hunnicutt's fair-haired boy, and he didn't like it in the slightest that Libby had been chosen in his place. He'd made it vociferously clear that he was better qualified, had seniority, et cetera. If Libby knew him, and she did, he'd still be blustering and protesting.

And she couldn't necessarily blame him. She had no idea why Edward J. Hunnicutt had chosen her for his top-secret research project, and if the damned man ever decided to meet with her she had every intention of flat-out asking him.

It was almost dark by the time the limo pulled to a stop, and Libby blinked, wondering if jet lag had finally turned her brain to mush. She scrambled out of the back seat, into the dense, tropical heat, and stared upward in awe.

It was an impressive edifice, a fortress, all shiny and so new she could smell the lumber and fresh paint over the humid scent of the jungle behind them. It sprawled across the top of the bluff, and she realized belatedly that they'd been climbing higher and higher. It was too dark to know for certain, but she suspected they were at the highest point on the island, and if there were any windows in the place they'd look out over the entire area. There were no windows in the front.

"What is this place?" she asked the driver, who was busy hauling out her suitcases. He ignored her, starting up the front steps, and she had no choice but to follow him. She could see several separate buildings off to the left, almost hidden by the jungle growth, and those buildings looked just as new as this one. Someone had gone to a great deal of effort and expense to build this place. But then, expense was no object to someone like Edward J. Hunnicutt.

There was no handle on the front door, no window, no bell to announce arrivals. Nevertheless the door swung open silently as the chauffeur approached it, laden with her luggage, and she scrambled after him, her laptop clutched to her chest.

The door swung shut behind her, silently, and she found herself standing alone in a white, empty hallway. The chauffeur had disappeared, abandoning her in the air-conditioned stillness. She took a tentative step forward, and a light came on. She stepped back, and it went off. She tried it again, two steps forward, and more lights illuminated the hallway. Downright creepy, she decided, wondering if there was any way she could talk her silent driver into taking her back.

There was no way she was getting on another puddle jumper for the foreseeable future, and the mere thought of it was enough to stiffen her resolve. "Is anyone here?" she called out. She'd hoped her voice sounded brisk and professional, but there was a betraying wobble to it, and she cleared her throat, annoyed with herself.

"Right here, my dear." And Edward J. Hunnicutt himself appeared from a recessed doorway she hadn't even noticed was there, a faintly amused expression on his face. "Did you think we'd abandoned you?"

"I'm a bit jet-lagged," she said faintly, stalling for time. "I didn't know what to think."

She still didn't. She'd never seen the infamous Edward J. Hunnicutt in the flesh—he tended to be reclusive. Somehow she'd expected he'd be different.

She wasn't a very tall woman, but he wasn't much bigger than she was. She knew from her research that he was even younger than she was, and he'd amassed his astounding fortune through computers, but beyond that she didn't care. Finances bored her—the only use she had for numbers was to quantify scientific data. He wasn't a bad-looking man, nor particularly handsome. As a matter of fact, he was almost alarmingly average, with a bland, even-featured face, brown hair combed straight back from his high forehead, trim body neatly attired in a lightweight tropical suit. He didn't look like a computer geek, a financial wizard, or a multimillionaire. He didn't look like much of anything at all.

"You were very kind to drop everything and

come here at such short notice," he said, both of them ignoring the fact that it hadn't been a matter of choice. "I'm sure you'd like a chance to rest and freshen up, but I'm afraid I'm on a tight schedule, and if we're going to talk we'll have to do it now. I'm leaving in ten minutes."

She stared at him blankly. "Ten minutes?" *Take me with you,* she almost begged. Back to Richard's smirking face, to admit failure before she'd even started? Back to the tiny airplane? No. "Fine," she said briskly. "Where can we talk?"

He gestured into the room, and she preceded him, once more assaulted by the stark whiteness, the shocking newness of the place. No windows in the room, and little furniture—just two chairs and a small table. Hunnicutt took one, signaling for her to take the other.

It was surprisingly comfortable. She should have known that a man with his kind of money would spare no expense. "What am I doing here?" she asked. "What's this mysterious, important scientific discovery I've been brought to observe, and why all the secrecy? Why me?"

"In what order do you want me to answer your questions, my dear?" He sounded like an amused elderly uncle. He was three years younger than she was, she reminded herself testily. And at least three billion times richer. "I wanted you because of your particular qualifications. You have doctorates in both anthropology and linguistics, you're intelligent, unsentimental, unattached and reasonably ambitious. I've had my eye on you for quite some time now, and I've been most impressed. You aren't aware of it, but I've been behind most of the grant monies that have been supporting your work. I knew that sooner or later you'd be just the person I needed, and that time has come.''

If that was supposed to set her mind at rest, it failed dismally. She was certainly intelligent, and most definitely unattached. She wasn't so sure about the unsentimental or ambitious part, but she wasn't about to correct him. ''Why am I here?'' she said instead.

''To observe and document my discovery. I'm afraid Dr. McDonough had only begun when he met with his unfortunate accident.''

''Dr. McDonough? William McDonough was working on this when he was killed?'' She was astonished. William McDonough's death two months before had shocked the entire scientific community. He hadn't been well liked, but the man had been utterly brilliant, and there had been rumors of an astounding discovery just before he died. That discovery apparently had just fallen in her lap.

''An unfortunate car accident.'' Hunnicutt shrugged. ''Not one of my personal limousines, of course, nor one of my drivers. Since then I've made

certain that my associates are properly provided for.
It was a great loss to science, if not for mankind.''

No, not a loss for mankind, if half the stories
were true. ''And what was he working on?''

Hunnicutt smiled, the look of a pastry chef about
to present a perfect crème brûlée. ''Something ex-
traordinary.''

Libby had never been known for her patience,
and eighteen hours of jet lag didn't help matters.
''Didn't you have to leave in ten minutes?''

Hunnicutt blinked, obviously not used to being
rushed. And then he smiled again, this time a bit
more rigidly. ''There's a folder full of Dr. Mc-
Donough's notes in your rooms. That will give you
something to start with. I want everything docu-
mented, observed closely. Two of my men will be
assisting you, Brown and Droggan, and they'll
know how to get in touch with me in case of emergency. In the meantime, secrecy is of the utmost
importance. You know how it is in the scientific
world—if anyone had a notion of my discovery
we'd have people crawling all over this island.''

''I thought you owned it.''

''I do. That won't keep them away. We'll make
our announcement when the time is right and no
sooner. And the time won't be right until you've
finished your work.''

''My work on what?'' she demanded, frustrated.

"What did you discover? Dinosaur eggs? A lost tribe? Aliens?"

"Close," he said. "I've discovered a missing link."

She stared at him in disbelief. "Link? Between what? Don't tell me you've found some kind of Yeti or Sasquatch."

"Not quite. Tarzan might be a better choice."

"Tarzan," she said blankly, wondering if Hunnicutt had lost his mind.

"We found a wild child, Dr. Holden. A creature raised up in the jungle with no outside influence. Just think of the possibilities for research. They're endless, and you hold them all in your hands."

She looked down at her hands, still clutching her laptop case. Small, strong hands, ringless. "I want to see him."

"Of course you do," Hunnicutt said serenely. "And you will, once you read through the preliminary reports. Besides, you need time to get accustomed to the new time zone and climate. It's a far cry from Chicago in January, isn't it? The creature isn't going anywhere. We have him sedated, kept in a controlled environment, and a few more days won't matter."

"The creature?" she echoed, faintly horrified.

Hunnicutt shrugged. "McDonough called him Tarzan. I don't know what Droggan and Brown call him. I rather fancy something like the Lost Man, though in Latin or Greek. You can call him what you like, though perhaps a code name might come in handy. Let me think about it and I'll let you know.''

He rose. Clearly the interview was at an end, but Libby just stared up at him in annoyance. ''You haven't answered half my questions....''

''Dr. McDonough's research will take care of that. In the meantime, I really do have to leave. Droggan!''

He must have been lurking just out of sight. ''Yes, sir?'' A big, surprisingly normal-looking man appeared. One arm was in a cast, and he had a sweet, innocent round face.

''This is Dr. Holden. I expect you and Brown to take good care of her while I'm away, assist her in any way possible. She'll be in charge of our little project, with you in charge of security. I'm sure you'll manage to be as helpful to her as you are to me.''

''We'll do our best, sir.'' Cockney accent, Libby noticed.

''I'm not sure when I'll be back. It shouldn't be too long. You know how to get in touch with me if need be, but I don't expect any such need to arise. I do make myself clear, Droggan?''

''Like crystal, Mr. Hunnicutt. Have a good trip.''

Libby still hadn't moved from her chair, staring up at the two of them in mute dismay.

"Don't worry about anything, Dr. Holden. A few hours' sleep, a good meal, and everything will be right as rain. Mr. Droggan's associate, Mr. Brown, happens to be an excellent cook. The two of them will see to your every need."

Dismay changed to outright alarm. "Are we the only ones here?"

"The smaller the operation the better, don't you think? I don't want reporters catching wind of my little enterprise. We don't want to tip our hand, now, do we, hmm?"

"Come along, Dr. Holden," Droggan said in his kindly voice. "We'll get you all settled."

She followed him out into the barren hallway, then turned to ask one more question of Hunnicutt. The man had disappeared without a sound, without a trace.

Libby stared at the empty room, momentarily unnerved. And then she squared her shoulders in determination. "I'll need to call the States and tell them I've arrived," she said briskly.

"Mr. Hunnicutt will see to it," Droggan said calmly, starting down the corridor, the lights automatically preceding him.

"I'd like to talk to my colleagues...."

"No outside communication, I'm afraid. Mr. Hunnicutt won't allow it. There's no phone, no computer modem, nothing."

Again that strange feeling of being trapped. "But I have people I need to call...."

"Mr. Hunnicutt chose you because you had no family, miss. All the other qualified candidates had connections, responsibilities."

"You mean the others had a life," she said bitterly.

"Lucky you, miss. You get the chance the others missed."

"Lucky me," she echoed.

"You'll like your rooms, Dr. Holden. Old Ed spared no expense."

"Old Ed?" she echoed, aghast.

"That's what Mick and I call him. The man was born old, don't you think?"

"Mr. Droggan—"

"Call me Alf. We might as well be chummy."

The last thing she wanted was to get chummy with someone like Alf Droggan. For all his sweet face, there was something in his eyes that made her uneasy.

"I'm really tired, Mr. Droggan...."

"Of course you are, love," he said. "And here you are." The handleless door opened, like something out of *Star Trek,* and Libby looked inside.

"See," Alf said, sounding pleased. "Just the way you like it. Do you want to eat first or have a nap?"

"I'm not hungry," Libby said dazedly.

"Well, when you decide you are just press the call button on the intercom, and either Mick or I will answer. Welcome to Ghost Island, Dr. Holden."

He was gone before she could respond, the door swooshing shut. It was a good thing—she wasn't sure what she'd be able to say.

She took a few steps forward, set the computer on the floor and collapsed into the oak mission chair with the leather seat cushion. She glanced at the oak armrest. No, it wasn't hers—there was a scar in the wood of the right arm of her chair, made long before she'd bought it at a flea market. This arm was unblemished.

She looked up, at the round oak table that was a duplicate to the one in her apartment. The Oriental carpet beneath her feet was newer than hers, less worn, but a perfect match. The prints on the walls, the vase filled with dried flowers, the stereo system were all duplicates. And she knew if she rose and went into the adjoining room she'd find a copy of her bedroom furniture, down to the same Laura Ashley sheets.

A cold sweat covered her body. Someone had been in her apartment, carefully cataloged her possessions. There was probably even a copy of *Great Expectations* on the side table. She'd made it her New Year's resolution to try to appreciate Charles Dickens, but so far it had been a losing battle.

No telephone. She reached down and opened her briefcase, pulling out the tiny cell phone she always kept with her. She turned it on, staring at the ominous Out of Range message on the screen. They were deep in some sort of bunker—that didn't mean it wouldn't work if she could ever find her way outside of this air-conditioned prison. It would probably be better if Alf and the unseen Mick didn't know she had it. One never knew when something like this might come in handy.

She rose, peering inside the bedroom at the copies of her familiar furniture. She used the bathroom, with the thick cotton towels just a faint shade off from her lavender ones, and opened the medicine chest. Everything a girl might need, including condoms. Who did they think she was going to use them with? She slammed it shut again.

She ran a hand through her short, curly blond hair. She looked just like she usually looked after a nineteen-hour plane ride. Pale, exhausted, circles under her blue eyes, no lipstick on her full mouth. Richard had always told her she could be very pretty if she put a little effort into it. Such flattery didn't do much to endear him to her.

She was pretty enough. Too short, too flat-chested, with five pounds she could do without, but then, what woman didn't want to get rid of five pounds? She had good skin, good teeth, pretty eyes and average features. Her parents had thought she was beautiful, but then, that's what parents were for. Once they died there was no one to tell her she was clever and pretty and wonderful. And she'd almost forgotten anyone ever thought it.

The files lay on the oak table, beckoning. She was too tired to think, too tired to sleep. In the windowless rooms she felt claustrophobic, and she knew the only cure for that sense of panic was work.

She sat down and opened the folder, staring in disbelief at the black-and-white photo of Dr. McDonough's Tarzan.

ALF WALKED INTO the observation room and sat down beside Mick, breathing a heavy sigh. "What's up, then?" he asked, nodding toward the two-way mirror.

"He's out like a lamb, as always. It's been dead boring, sitting here staring at him. I was thinking we might poke him a bit, see if he responded..."

"You aren't being paid to think, Mick," Alf said.

"Good thing, too," said Mick cheerfully. That was one good thing about Mick—he had no delusions about his mental processes, Alf thought. "So tell me about the new doctor. What's she look like? Think she'll be better than McDonough?"

"Couldn't be much worse," Alf observed. "Depends on what you mean, though. I think Old Ed might have made a mistake this time."

"Why do you always call him Old Ed? He's younger than we are."

"I like to," Alf said.

Mick wisely decided not to question him further on that. "So what about Dr. Holden? Why would it be a mistake?"

Alf shook his head. "I dunno. Call me superstitious," he said, knowing perfectly well Mick would never be impertinent enough to do so. "I just think she's going to be her own brand of trouble. And I have to admit, laddie, that I'm not in the mood for that kind of trouble." He shook his head. "Not in the mood at all."

Chapter Two

He dreamed. There wasn't much else he could do, trapped in his motionless body. The memories flew by, tangled like the vines surrounding him, wrapping him tightly, too tightly to move. He was choking, the vines wrapped around his throat, and he couldn't fight back, couldn't rip them away. He tried to call out, but there was only silence, the words stolen from him on a whirlwind, and his breath followed after them, so that he was struggling, clawing for air.

Even opening his eyes required too much effort. He was lost in a thick black fog, and every time he thought it might be lifting he could hear the voices, feel the sharp sting against his skin, and he'd sink back into oblivion.

Every now and then he could remember bits and pieces, tumbled together, but the days and weeks and years blurred together. He remembered the men coming out of nowhere, the bite of the rope around his neck, the words he couldn't understand as he tried to fight back. He remembered other things as well, things he didn't want to dwell on. Burying the bodies with his bare hands, listening to the sound of the jungle all around him, warning him, watching him.

He had no idea who he was, where he was, when he was. He was lost, trapped in a fog created by strange men, and he couldn't escape.

LIBBY WOKE SUDDENLY, ripped from sleep with a violence that left her trembling, disoriented, and it took her countless moments to realize where she was.

She'd fallen asleep at the table in her creepily replicated cell, her face pressed against the stacks of paper and photos that the late Dr. McDonough had left behind. She had no idea how long she'd slept, only that her body felt cramped and stiff and someone was knocking at the door.

With a stifled moan she pushed back from the table, rising on unsteady legs. The photos lay scattered on the table, and for some odd reason she quickly shuffled them back together, tucking them inside the folder, before she went to the door.

Fat lot of good that it did here. There was no handle, doorknob, no visible way to open it. "Who's there?" she called out.

"Mick Brown, Dr. Holden. I've brought you something to eat. May I come in?"

Another Cockney accent, like his associate's, Mr. Droggan. "I don't have any idea how to open the door," she said.

Immediately the white door slid open, not improving Libby's sense of security one whit. Standing in front of her was a small, ferret-faced man with clever, malicious eyes and an unlikely smile. "There's a button hidden in the casement, miss," he said. "To the left there."

She ran her hand along the side of the door until she found it. She pushed, and the door slid shut in the man's face. A moment later he opened it again.

"See," he said cheerfully. "Simple as pie."

"Is there any way to lock it?"

The man looked oddly stricken. "Why would you want to do that, miss? It's safe as houses around here. We've got the ape-man locked up all tight and proper, and there's only me and me mate Alf here. No one here to harm you."

For some reason the villainous-looking man's feelings were hurt. "I just like a sense of privacy," she said in an apologetic tone.

"No place more private. Alf and me live on the lower level, beneath the observation area, and you're alone on this floor. You can walk around starkers for all the notice anyone would pay you."

"That's not the point. I find it difficult to con-

centrate on my work if I think I might be interrupted.''

"But we wouldn't…"

"I need a lock, Mr. Brown," she said firmly.

He shrugged, defeated. "No problem, Dr. Holden. Alf can adjust it on the computer that runs the
household. It'll just take him a minute."

"That relieves my mind," Libby said dryly, but
Mick Brown didn't even notice her sarcasm.

"You must be hungry, miss. I brought you some
chicken soup and a sandwich, just a little something
to tide you over. I don't know if Alf told you, but
you've got a refrigerator filled with juices and energy drinks. Dr. McDonough didn't usually bother
with food at all—the protein and vitamin shakes got
him through."

"I like food," Libby said firmly, taking the tray
from him. He wasn't much taller than she was,
though a little taller than Edward J. Hunnicutt.
"What time is it? I forgot to change my watch."

"I don't think you're going to want to bother
with that, miss. After all, time is relative out
here…."

"Part of scientific observation is to keep accurate
records, and I can hardly do that without a watch,
now, can I?"

"It's half past three, miss."

"That's not too bad," she said. "Er…is that
morning or afternoon?"

"Middle of the night, miss. But don't you worry—you'll get used to it soon enough."

She had her doubts about that. "When can I see my subject?"

"No hurry, miss. He's been waiting this long. He'll keep a few hours longer, just while you get a chance to eat something and tidy up a bit."

"I'll be ready to inspect the facilities in fifteen minutes," she said firmly.

"Now, miss, we just gave George his shot. He won't even be moving for hours now."

"Shot?"

"A very special concoction of cutting-edge tranquilizers. They keep him sedated without interfering with his blood. He gets it every four hours. Keeps 'im nice and docile. Dr. McDonough was having us cut back when Alf had his little accident, so we thought it best to up the dosage again. Safer all around."

"Safer?" she echoed.

"He gets a bit too frisky if we don't dope him up. Broke Alf's arm in three places. The bruises are just starting to heal."

"Mr. Droggan didn't look bruised."

"No, on the ape-man, miss. Alf's got a nasty streak when he's crossed, and he took it out on old Tarzan, he did."

"His name isn't Tarzan."

"Well, that's as good a name as any. Sometimes

we call 'im George of the Jungle, especially after Alf got through with him. Looked like he'd gone splat into a tree. Old Ed calls him the Creature, but that makes me think of the *Black Lagoon* movie, and this thing didn't come from no swamp.''

''We'll find a name for him. In the meantime, I'll be ready to see the...subject in half an hour. Why don't you see if you can do something about the lock?'' She kept her tone firm.

Mick shrugged. ''Anything you say, Doc. I'll be back in a jiff.''

The door slid shut behind him, and Libby stayed where she was, holding the tray in her hands. Belatedly she realized the steaming soup smelled delicious, and she set the tray down on the table, away from the folder that someone had titled Project: Missing Link.

She ate quickly, efficiently, took a fast shower and put on fresh clothes: khakis, a polo shirt and a white lab coat. She didn't usually wear a lab coat, but right now she wanted the security of it. Her hair was still wet when she heard the rapping on her door, but it was so short she just shook it dry as she went to answer it.

She followed Mick down the long, spotless hallways, listening to his chatter with only half a brain as she tried to pick out almost nonexistent landmarks. She'd find her way back to her room, but not without a bit of trouble. "How long has this place been here?" she asked.

Mick grinned at her. "You wouldn't believe it. Not much more than a couple of months. Old Ed can get what he wants, when he wants, with the kind of money he has. Before that this island belonged to a group of multinational ecological organizations, but once they found Tarzan old Ed swooped in and bought it, lock, stock and rain forest. Had this place erected in record time, he did, and we've been here ever since, keeping an eye on things, so to speak."

"Is there anyone else on the island?"

"Nope. It was supposedly uninhabited, until Tarzan…er, the subject was discovered. Then Hunnicutt took over, and the rest is history."

"Actually I'd say the rest is top secret, considering there isn't even a telephone line out here," Libby said. "What's he so paranoid about?"

"Afraid someone will scoop him when it comes to his big discovery. Old Ed's a determined man, and he doesn't like coming in second. I think he's looking for the Nobel Prize."

"Bankers aren't usually the ones who get the prizes," she said dryly. "Just because he's funding the research doesn't mean he's earned the award."

"Ed has a way of getting what he wants. And dangling the right sort of rewards in front of those he needs to help him. You'd like to be involved in a prize-winning scientific discovery, now, wouldn't you? It would make your career—you could write your own ticket."

"Yes," she said, always honest.

"Everyone's got a price," Mick said cheerfully, pausing before a double door. "And Ed's willing to meet it."

The doors slid open, exposing a huge room that looked like a white-painted mission control from the NASA space center. Rows of desks, computer screens and technical instruments, beeping noises, formed a semicircle around a huge screen. The main difference was the almost total lack of manpower. Only Alf Droggan was in the room, leaning against one of the desks as he stared into the screen.

He stood up, slowly, with just a trace of hesitation, and nodded his balding head. "Welcome to the fish tank, Dr. Holden. Did you have a nice nap?"

Lying facedown on an oak table was not Libby's idea of a nice nap, but she nodded. "Who was responsible for my rooms?"

"Something wrong with them?" Mick asked anxiously.

"No, they're fine. They're just a little too...familiar."

Alf laughed, a hearty, booming sound that belied his cool, watching eyes. "It's a mistake to underestimate Hunnicutt, Dr. Holden. He can do anything he wants. I presume he somehow managed to make your rooms here look like your current apartment.''

''How'd you guess?''

''He gave us that choice. Considering that our digs here are a hell of a lot nicer than the ones we were used to, we said no thanks. But he must have decided to just go ahead and have yours done, anyway.''

''But I don't understand how he managed it.''

''He can manage anything he bloody well pleases. We're talking about the seventh-richest man in the world here, and for what it's worth, I bet he's closer to number one than anyone would guess. He doesn't have limits.''

''He has legal and moral limits,'' Libby said, glancing at the blank screen.

''Not so's you'd notice,'' Alf said, following her gaze. ''You want to see our ape-man?''

''She doesn't want to call him that. Not Tarzan, nor George of the Jungle,'' Mick said hastily. ''We're to call him…what did you say?''

''The subject,'' Libby said. ''Until we come up with something more appropriate.''

''Call him what you will, love. He's George of the Jungle to me. Been dancing with a few too many trees of late.'' He flexed his casted arm.

''Where is he?''

''Take a gander, love.'' He leaned across the desk and pushed a switch, and the screen was no longer a screen, it was a huge window, illuminating a tangled overgrowth of jungle vegetation. She moved closer, staring into the tangled thicket.

"You let him run free?" she asked.

"Not usually. And he doesn't run anywhere, Doc. He's flat on his back, doped to the gills. There's nothing free about 'is little habitat. It's huge, but there are electrified fences all around the perimeter. No way he's getting out or anyone getting in without frying their bacon."

Alf Droggan sounded quite cheered by the thought, and Libby controlled an instinctive shudder. "How strong is the voltage? I don't think Mr. Hunnicutt would appreciate having his scientific discovery electrocuted."

"Don't you worry your pretty little head about that, miss. It's just strong enough to knock him out, maybe fry a few brain cells. It won't kill him. And as far as I can tell he doesn't have any brain cells to worry about."

"That's my job, isn't it?" Libby said coolly. "To figure out how many brain cells he has? I wouldn't want anything interfering with the data. I want him in his natural state—I don't want to have to take injuries into account."

"Bit too late for that, now, isn't it?" Alf said cheerfully. "The Russian hunters who captured him weren't particularly delicate with the creature. He was a right mess when he showed up, and he hasn't done much to endear himself to us in the meantime. He's a bit banged and bruised, but pretty much as they found him, I'd think.''

"I thought you kept him drugged all the time. Why is he banged and bruised?" Libby demanded.

Alf shrugged, the image of innocence. "Accidents do 'appen, don't they, love?''

If he called her love one more time she was going to scream. She took a deep breath. Scientific detachment, she reminded herself. Isn't that what Richard always said she lacked? She was too passionate about things—it muddied the data.

"Could I see him, please?" she said with deceptive calm.

"Use your eyes, Doc. He's there on the table."

She moved into the room, closer to the window, staring at the oppressive greenery. And then she saw him, lying still and motionless on what looked like a hospital gurney draped in camouflage sheets.

"Nice bed, don't you think?" Alf said with a smirk. "Ed wanted it color-coordinated."

But she was no longer paying attention to the broad Cockney voice ringing in her ear. All her attention was focused on the still figure of a man.

The pictures had been astonishing enough, but they failed to prepare her for the reality of Ed Hunnicutt's wild man.

He was beautiful. There was no other word for him. Beneath the tangle of long, dark hair, beneath the deeply tanned skin and rough beard, he was absolutely stunning. She let her eyes run down the entire length of his body, his lean, muscled shoulders and chest, his long legs ending in bare, narrow feet. He was wearing some sort of ragged cutoffs and nothing else, and he looked like the male equivalent of Sleeping Beauty, perfection lost in an endless sleep.

His face had been bruised and misshapen in the photographs, but now she could see only the occasional marks of abuse, the bluish-yellow of fading bruises, the faint puffiness by one of his eyes. She stared at him in awe and fascination, silent, wondering.

"Quite the pretty boy, isn't he?" Alf said with a snicker. "That's how the Russians heard of him. The Abo's said there was a beautiful god on this island, and they came out to check and bagged him."

"Abo's?"

"Aborigines. Natives. They used to come hunt on this island, and they must have run across him at some point or another. 'Course, they don't come anywhere near here now that Old Ed owns it. He's got the place mined."

That was enough to distract her. "You're kidding!"

"Not very big mines," Mick said hastily. "They

cause more noise than damage, really. And no one's stupid enough to try to come here anymore."

"Or try to leave," Alf said casually.

"Come here and look at this screen, Doc," Mick said, casting a worried glance at his partner. "You won't believe what that bed really does."

"Provide electroshock therapy?" she suggested sharply.

"That's a good one, Doc!" Alf's laughter rumbled through his big frame. "I wish I'd thought of it."

"Dr. Holden might not know you're kidding, Alf," Mick said in a warning voice.

Dr. Holden knows he's not kidding, Libby said to herself. She moved to the screen, staring down at the blinking numbers.

"It registers everything, when he's lying down there," Mick said. "His weight, blood pressure, heart rate."

"It'll even tell you when he passes gas," Alf joined in.

Libby ignored him. "His vital signs are low," she said, peering at the screen.

"Yours would be, too, if you were pumped full of drugs," Alf said. "He's lost some weight since he's been here—down to one hundred and ninety, but that's because he won't usually eat what we feed him."

"What does he eat, then?"

"Fruits, berries, stuff that's growing there. I think he's afraid we'll drug the food."

"I can't imagine why," Libby said dryly. "When's he due for his next shot?"

"Not for another couple of hours. Why?"

"Give him half the dosage."

"I don't think so," Alf said.

She turned to give him her most intimidating stare, the one that never failed to put terror into the hearts of research assistants. Unfortunately Alf Droggan was almost a foot taller than she was and probably weighed two-and-a-half times what she did, and the effort fell short.

"I'm in charge of the subject," she said sternly. "And I say you lower his dosage."

"And I'm in charge of security, little lady, and I say he gets the full dose. He wakes up enough every now and then for you to poke and prod him and see how he reacts—that's good enough."

"I can't do my work…"

"Take it up with Mr. Hunnicutt."

"And how am I expected to do that when he's left and there are no telephones on this island?" she demanded, running a hand through her short, damp hair.

"I'll mention your concerns to him," Alf said sweetly. "And I'll let you know what he has to say."

Libby took another deep, calming breath.

"Fine," she said with deceptive good humor. "In the meantime, I'd like to see our subject."

"Look all you like."

"No, I mean see him. Up close and personal. If he's so drugged, he won't even know I'm there. How do we get in there?"

"I wouldn't suggest..." Alf began.

"I'm not asking for your suggestions, Mr. Droggan," Libby said crisply. "I'm here to do a job and I intend to do it. I want to go in there and check him out myself."

Alf Droggan rolled his eyes, letting out a long-suffering sigh. "You heard her, Mick," he said. "Might as well get out the guns."

Chapter Three

"Guns?" Libby echoed in unfeigned horror.

"Tranquilizer guns, miss," Mick said reassuringly. "Just as a precaution. Tarzan...er...the subject is a big, strong man, and it's hard to calibrate the proper dosage. We thought he was out cold when he managed to break Alf's arm, and I'd hate to think what he could do to a little-bitty thing like you."

Libby had never been particularly fond of the fact that she was only five feet one inch tall, but she was coming to recognize Mick's essential sweetness, so she bit back her protest. "All right," she said. "But I don't want the two of you interfering unless it's an emergency. And I'll be the one to decide whether it's an emergency or not. Understood?"

"Completely," Alf said amiably, but Libby wasn't fooled for a minute.

She waited, impatient, staring at the still form of her subject, while Alf and Mick argued about tranquilizer darts. He didn't move, barely seemed to breathe, and she wondered just how drugged he was. Whether he knew he was being watched, constantly, by people who'd basically taken him prisoner. Did he long for freedom, did he hate captivity?

"Ready, miss?" Alf was standing by the door leading into the observation area, a nasty-looking gun in his meaty hand. It certainly looked like it shot bullets, not tranquilizer darts, but she had to trust that Alf would know better than to seriously damage his employer's prize trophy.

"Ready," she said.

The heat and humidity beyond the sliding metal door were a momentary assault on her senses, but Libby didn't hesitate, stepping into the jungle with Mick and Alf close behind her.

Whoever had built this place had done a masterful job. The wall was camouflaged, festooned with vines and plants, and the other side of the observation window was some sort of mesh camouflage, unnoticeable unless you were looking for it. In the dim, shadowy light she couldn't see the fences that had to surround the place, and she glanced back at Alf.

"How much room does he have?"

"Three bloody acres fenced in, which is ridiculous if you ask me. The poor sod barely moves as it is—why Hunnicutt had to have such a huge playground built for him is beyond my way of thinking. It was close enough to his natural habitat, but no, they had to bring in more trees and plants, more rocks. It's ridiculous.''

"Does he realize that you've drugged the subject?''

"'Course he does. What do you think he does when he's here? He sits and stares at Tarzan like he held the answers to the secrets of the universe.''

"Maybe he does.''

"Yeah, and maybe my Aunt Fanny...'' Alf growled. "You want to get this over with? You might still be in a different time zone, but it's the middle of the night for us.''

She ignored him, moving toward the camouflage gurney with its still, silent occupant. Up close he was even more impressive—long arms and legs and torso, with the kind of subtle musculature that suggested speed and strength. He was wearing some sort of shorts instead of a fur loincloth, but that didn't lessen the hint of savagery about his still figure.

His dark hair was long, matted and probably crawling with bugs, she thought. He was very tanned, the kind of deep bronze color that comes from years, decades of sun exposure. She moved closer, looking into his face. The beard was short, scruffy, the nose sharp and strong. Neither his jaw nor his brow were protruding, though both were strong and well formed. She couldn't get a good idea of his mouth beneath the beard, but she could see the bruised swelling beside his left eye, almost hidden by the long hair. She let her gaze slide down his body. Some body hair, but not excessive amounts. There were bruises along his side, some aging and yellowed, some newer, darker blues and purples over his ribs.

"Did you kick him, Alf?" she asked in a steady voice, not bothering to look around.

"Only when he was already knocked out," Mick said earnestly. "He wouldn't have felt a thing."

Alf snorted with laughter, obviously not worried about Libby's reaction. "You tell 'er, lad," he said.

"Don't do it again." Libby's voice was as cold as ice.

"If he comes at me—"

"You might have cracked his ribs. They could puncture a vital organ, he'd bleed to death internally, and Edward J. Hunnicutt would have spent a great deal of money with absolutely nothing to show for it. I wouldn't want to be the one to explain that to him. Would you?"

She still didn't bother to look at Alf, knowing by the silence that she'd made her point. The gurney was waist-high, and she knew she had to touch the man lying there, but for some reason she was reluctant to, particularly with Hunnicutt's two minions watching her. However, they were unlikely to leave her, and she needed to see if she could tell what kind of damage Alf's boots had wrought.

The touch of his skin beneath her fingers was a shock, and it took all her concentration not to jerk her hand away. He was warm. Pliant. Resilient. *What else did you expect, Libby?* She mocked herself. *It's simply a human being. Living flesh is pretty much the same.*

And she was lying to herself. His living flesh was a far cry from the tender skin of a baby, from the burly brutality of Alf Droggan's bearlike skin, from Edward J. Hunnicutt's soft, pampered body. It was a far cry from her own smooth, sensitive flesh. It was heat and power, strength and endurance. And it wasn't "it." It was he. Male, masculine.

"Does he understand English?" she asked over her shoulder.

"He doesn't understand a blooming thing—even when he's not out of it, he just stands there staring like he's lost his wits," Alf said. "Not that I think he ever had any in the first place."

"Do you talk to him?"

"Why should I? It's a waste of time."

"He needs to learn to communicate. He needs to get used to the sound of voices, to the sound of words. That's how babies learn to talk—by listening to their mothers."

"Well, coo all you want over 'im," Alf said. "I don't think he's got the wits to learn anything, and I don't know if he could speak even if he wanted to. All he does is growl."

"And who can blame you?" Libby muttered under her breath. She touched the bruised skin on his side, trying to feel if the ribs were in place, trying to ignore the heat emanating from him. She realized she'd been holding her breath, and she let it out suddenly.

He jerked reflexively beneath her probing fingers, and she jumped back, startled, but his eyes didn't open, and he stilled again.

She pushed the hair away from the swollen bruise by his eyes. He'd have a scar there once it healed, but there were scars all over his body, most of them ancient. Scars from cuts and tears that had never been treated with stitches or butterfly bandages or any of the accoutrements of modern medicine.

"But what should I expect?" she said in a quiet undertone. "Wherever you've been, wherever you've lived your life, there's been no one around to take care of you. Can you even talk at all?"

"What are you muttering about?" Alf demanded suspiciously, moving closer.

"I'm talking to myself. And to the subject. And keep your distance, please. I don't want him opening his eyes and seeing you. I could be wrong, but

I'm guessing the sight of you doesn't fill him with a sense of well-being.''

"He should have learned his lesson by now, if that's what you mean," Alf said with an air of satisfaction. "Not that he has. Tarzan here doesn't surrender easily."

"Do you think he'd still be alive after years in the wild if he was the type to surrender?" she said sharply. "And don't call him Tarzan."

"What do you want me to call him, your ladyship? Bloody Prince Charming?"

It's a start, she thought, and a faint blush washed over her. Not *her* Prince Charming, of course. But someone's.

She ignored Alf's taunt. "You know, he's out like a light. There's no need for you to hover around with your hand on your weapon like some Western gunslinger. He's not going to wake up and he's not going to hurt me. Why don't you go back into the observation room and let me work in peace? I promise to scream if he even twitches."

"And just what kind of work were you planning on doing, Doc?" Alf laughed wheezily. "We don't mind watching as you run your hands all over him. I'm just wondering what else you're planning to touch."

"You're disgusting, Mr. Droggan," she said calmly. "And since you're so interested in being helpful, why don't you go back and bring a clipboard and take notes of my observations?''

"I'm no bloody secretary. There's a tape recorder for that sort of thing. Hunnicutt's got a voice recognition machine that'll type it out for you."

She turned her head to look at him. "Then go get me the tape recorder, Mr. Droggan."

There was a moment's silence as a battle of wills was fought over the unconscious body between them. "Anything you say, miss," Alf said finally. "Come along, Mick. If Dr. Holden thinks she can handle the ape-man herself, so be it."

It took her a moment to realize she was alone with him, the door sealing them in together in the steamy heat of the manufactured rain forest. She had nothing to worry about, she reminded herself. Droggan and Mick weren't that far away, and she had no doubt they were watching and listening avidly.

She looked down at the bruised face of her subject. No, not her subject. Not some alien "it" to be prodded and poked. Him. Most definitely masculine, most definitely human, most definitely him.

Richard had always said that was her worst failing as a scientist. "Your wretched identification with your test subjects. They're data, nothing more. You'll never make the top echelon if you don't learn to disassociate."

She sighed. She'd learned to disassociate from

Richard, at least, which was a step in the right direction. But it was hard to be objective when the subject under her examination was a living, breathing, potent male.

"So what am I going to call you?" she said under her breath, her voice low and soothing, getting him used to it. His eyelids twitched for a moment, making her think his brain had at least registered the sound, even though the words would mean nothing for now. "There's no way you're going to be Tarzan or George of the Jungle or Ape-man. For one thing, you don't look like an ape, or any kind of prehistoric link. I don't know if Hunnicutt's hoping you'll be some sort of genetic freak, but you definitely have evolved bone structure. If anything, your face looks..." She peered down, trying to look at him beneath the bruises, the beard, the tangled hair. "I don't know what your face looks like," she said finally. "I'd like to see you without the beard, but I doubt if Laurel and Hardy are going to let me near you with a razor, and I wouldn't want either of them trying. If I know Alf he's more likely to cut your throat than your beard."

He was breathing, slow and steady, his chest rising and falling, and she touched the bruise on his cheekbone with the lightest of touches. He moaned, a harsh, strangled sound from the back of his throat, and then was still again.

"So you're not mute," she said quietly. "And

you can feel pain no matter how much stuff they pump in your veins. So what am I going to call you? Something ridiculous would probably be good for my piece of mind. Something like Elvis or Algernon.''

She wouldn't have been surprised if he'd stirred in protest, but he lay still. ''Adam wouldn't be bad. For the first man, you know. But you don't strike me as an Adam.''

''Call 'im John,'' Mick suggested, appearing beside her with no warning. ''It's a common-enough name. Here's your tape recorder.'' He handed her a minicassette recorder that looked as if it were made of titanium. It probably was.

''John,'' Libby echoed. ''I like that. Simple, short, with no emotional baggage attached to it. Thank you, Mick. We'll call him John.'' She clicked the record button and began her inventory. ''The subject, who shall be called John, is approximately six feet one inch tall—''

''Two.'' Alf's voice came over the intercom. She glanced up, but she could see nothing beyond the camouflaged screen. ''He's six two and one-quarter. We've got all those records already.''

''A scientist doesn't rely on someone else's data, Mr. Droggan,'' she said sternly. She clicked on the tape recorder again. ''He appears to be in excellent physical shape apart from some bruising along his left rib cage and a cut under his right eye. He has scars on his legs...two-and-half centimeters on the front of his lower left calf, seven centimeters on his right thigh. His feet are callused and consistent with years of being shoeless. There doesn't appear to be any flaccidity in his musculature, any atrophy despite the fact that he's been kept essentially motionless for the last..." She clicked the pause button on the recorder. "How long has he been here, Mick?"

Mick was perched on a rock nearby, watching with interest. "Almost three months, miss."

"Three months," she continued into the recorder. "He's being kept on a gurney, with arm restraints and large amounts of an experimental drug to keep him under control. I see no sign of birth trauma to suggest he might have been born in the wilderness, but I can't rule that out...." A sudden thought struck her, and she clicked off the recorder, turning to Mick. "Is he circumcised?"

She heard Alf's roar of laughter over the speaker. "Why don't you check him yourself, Doc? I thought you said you didn't trust anyone else's observation when you were right at hand."

She willed herself not to blush. She was a scientist, someone who prided herself on cool, dispassionate observation. "Very well," she said, reaching for the waistband of his shorts.

"Don't tease her, Alf," Mick said sternly. "He hasn't been cut, miss."

Without betraying her relief she let her hands drop and began transcribing again. "He looks to be about in his mid-twenties, though that could be deceptive. He could look younger than his actual age due to lack of exposure to pollutants and modern food, or he could appear prematurely aged due to the harsh life he's lived. At this point I'll estimate him to be twenty-five, and will probably adjust that when I've had more time to observe and perhaps communicate."

"He's not going to communicate with you, Dr. Holden," Mick said earnestly. "Even when he's not doped up he just glares at people, not reacting to a thing they say. Dr. McDonough thought he might be deaf, but he ruled that out. He just can't understand a bloody thing anyone says."

"Can't? Or won't?" she said serenely.

"You can lead a horse to water but you can't make 'im drink," Alf said over the speaker.

She looked toward the screen, narrowing her gaze at the unseen bully behind it. "Mr. Droggan, if you don't have anything helpful to add, would you please be quiet? I'm trying to concentrate on my observations. Why don't you go to bed and leave Mick here if you don't think I'd be safe alone? Though with the way you've got him tied up and doped up it would take nothing short of a miracle to get him to move."

"Sorry, Doc," Alf said, sounding not the slightest bit regretful. "Our orders are not to leave you alone with Tarzan here."

"John," she said firmly. "His name is John. And whose orders are those?"

"Mr. Hunnicutt's. We don't want another accident, now, do we?"

"Another accident? What are you talking about?"

"We don't want to lose another scientist just because we weren't careful enough."

"Are you telling me that he killed Dr. McDonough? That's ridiculous! Dr. McDonough died in a car crash. I read his obituary."

"Of course, miss," Alf's voice replied. "Whatever you say. Just remember you're dealing with Edward J. Hunnicutt. He can cover up anything he wants to cover up."

She turned to look at Mick in shock, but Mick merely shrugged, his narrow face blank.

She picked up the recorder again, hoping no one would notice the faint tremor in her hand, in her voice. "The subject, John, appears to be scarred and bruised from his difficult life, but in no way appears dangerous. His hands and feet are long and narrow, well-formed, and there's a jagged scar on his forehead near his hairline that may account for some brain trauma. He also has..." She turned to

Mick accusingly. "Oh, my God, what happened to his throat?"

"Neither of us did it, miss," Mick replied instantly. "It was like that when they brought him into us. I think they might have put a rope around his neck when they captured him."

She stared down at the marks on his strong neck in horror. "It looks like they tried to hang him."

"Oh, they wouldn't have done that, Doc," Mick said. "They knew his value the moment they found him. They might have strung him up for a bit to teach him a lesson, but they wouldn't have wanted to kill him. Those Russians are a rough lot but they like their money. They were probably just a bit overenthusiastic with him."

"And then he got into yours and Alf's clutches."

"I haven't hurt him, miss!" he said. "And Alf's only kicked him when he's been provoked."

"Alf strikes me as a man who's easily provoked," she said, knowing he was listening.

"You got that right, girlie." His voice came back over the intercom. "Are you finished giving your little pet the once-over, or do you want me to turn him and strip him for you?"

She was suddenly exhausted. The heat and humidity of the artificial area closed down around her like a wet blanket, and the hours of traveling caught up with her. "I'll finish my initial report tomorrow," she said. "In the meantime, I want you to unfasten his arm restraints."

"Not on your life, girlie. I'm not going in there with him roaming free."

"You can't keep him chained to the gurney all the time, Mr. Droggan," she said sharply.

"I don't. I let him loose on occasion. He gets his exercise, trust me. Tell you what, I'll compromise. I'll lower his dosage just a tiny bit so you can see what he's like when you come by tomorrow. Then maybe you'll think twice about letting him roam free all the time."

It was more than she'd hoped for. "It's possible. I'm sure I'll feel better after a few hours' rest, and I'm eager to get started on him."

"I wouldn't be too eager if I were you," Mick muttered. "He's a pain in the arse. Besides, we've got the life of Riley here. Anything you want, Hunnicutt will get. Newest movies, any food you could possibly want, books, telly. What more could you ask?"

"Civilization. I like cities."

"Well, that's where you differ from Tar...er, John. He's never seen a city in his life, I expect, and it would scare the crap out of him if he did."

"Then it's a good thing I'm not planning to take him to the city."

"Hunnicutt is."

She turned to stare at him. "What do you mean?"

"Well, he's hardly likely to release him to the wild again, now, is he? He's going to take him around the world and show him off. For all I know he might even breed him."

"Breed him? He's a man, not an animal!" she protested, shocked.

"He's both. And Mr. Hunnicutt could do anything he pleases. Everyone's got a price, and he could find a womb for rent easier than most. You haven't looked at the lab reports on his blood, have you? I don't understand half of it, but Dr. Mc-Donough's findings were...what did he say, Alf?"

Alf's voice drifted back over the speaker. "Significant, Mick. He said the findings were significant."

"Then why the hell am I here?" Libby demanded. "I'm an anthropology and linguistics expert with a premed background. You need people trained in hematology and biology and neurology."

"Oh, they'll come, miss. You're only the second in a long line of experts who are going to get a piece of John, there," Alf's disembodied voice was sepulchral.

"Good," Libby said, telling herself she was relieved.

It wasn't until she was back in the silence of her

duplicate room, stretched out on the double bed, that she remembered that the first expert to view John had died.

And she felt a sudden shiver dance across her skin in the perfect temperature of her room.

Chapter Four

Someone had been there. He'd heard her voice, soft, low, oddly soothing, though he didn't have any idea what she was saying to him. She touched his body, her fingers gentle on his side, against his skin. When she touched his face he jerked away from her, instinctively wary. But she simply murmured to him, those meaningless words, as her sensitive fingertips brushed his body.

He lay on the thing they'd strapped him to and breathed, breathed in the rich scent of her. He could pick out the smells quite easily, soap and shampoo and other artificial fragrances, covering up the clean, sweet scent of a female.

He heard the other voices, too, the ones that accompanied pain. She was part of them, and he couldn't trust her. She was keeping him tied up, just as they were, and she would hurt him, just as they had. It didn't matter that her voice was soft and soothing, that she smelled sweet and female. She was one more jailer, one more stranger to trap him. He couldn't forget that, couldn't lower his guard.

He made a low, growling noise in the back of his throat. It was the best he could do—it felt as if a huge fist had caught his throat in an iron grip. He could breathe better now—in the beginning he'd been afraid he'd suffocate. But he still couldn't do more than growl.

He flexed his hands surreptitiously. They were always watching him—he knew it with instincts honed from years in the jungle. They'd come with another shot before long, and he'd be out again.

But maybe this time he'd fight it a little longer. Long enough to open his eyes and see the woman they'd brought here. The woman who smelled so good.

LIBBY HAD NIGHTMARES. It shouldn't have surprised her—she was thousands of miles away from her home, yet surrounded by familiar things, and she had a wicked case of jet lag. It was little wonder she'd dreamed of a wild man chasing a small car down a twisting road, catching it with his strong hands and flinging it over his head into the chasm.

She sat up, and the lights came on, illuminating the familiar-unfamiliar room. It was as ridiculous as most dreams were, she reminded herself. John might be very strong, but there was no way any human could pick up an automobile and fling it over his head.

The car had been her brand-new VW Beetle, safely garaged back in Chicago. But she wasn't the scientist trapped inside, screaming to get out as he was flung to his death. It was Dr. McDonough.

She shivered in the perfect temperature, sliding her feet out of the bed. It was a perfectly understandable dream, she told herself. McDonough had died in a car wreck, plummeting off a cliff somewhere in Australia. Alf had tried to tell her John was responsible, so it was an obvious connection her subconscious had made. Throw in the fact that her apartment had been duplicated without her knowledge, and it was no wonder she'd dreamed her car had been here as well.

Unless, of course, she was dreaming that John would kill her as well.

Ridiculous, she said under her breath. There was no reason to think John would want to hurt anybody. Except Alf, with his broken arm. But then, she wouldn't be surprised if Alf had been deliberately hurting him. Who could blame John for fighting back when he was kept tied up, in pain, trapped after what was presumably a lifetime of freedom?

But wasn't she part and parcel of that entrapment? Did he have the understanding to realize the difference? For that matter, was there any difference? Edward J. Hunnicutt probably didn't kick him in the ribs with his boots, but he was the one who paid the bills that kept him prisoner. And she was there to observe and record, more ways to keep him trapped. He had every right to hate her as well.

He was too drugged up to hate anyone, but maybe she'd better think twice about having him roam free without tranquilizers, not when she was going to be in the room with him. A little bit at a time was the best answer. A little bit fewer drugs, a little bit more freedom, a little bit more access to him until she was sure he was harmless.

As harmless as Alf's broken arm.

She glanced at her watch. She'd set it before she fell into bed, but she still had no idea whether she'd slept twelve hours or twenty-four. It was a little after four.

She took a shower, hoping it would blast the fog out of her brain. This time she dressed in cooler clothes—if she was going to spend time in that jungle habitat she'd need to be more comfortable.

There was a refrigerator in one corner, and she opened it up on the off chance there might be a Diet Coke in there. She preferred Tab, but it was almost impossible to find, except at a small grocery store where they ordered it especially for her, and she had to make do with DC when she traveled.

She'd underestimated Ed Hunnicutt. The refrigerator was full of those familiar fuchsia cans, and she breathed a sigh of pure pleasure. For the right can of pop she was willing to forgive almost any transgression, including this mock apartment.

She drank down half of the can, ignoring the way it clashed with her toothpaste, and felt the delicious jump of caffeine and saccharine in her veins. It came as no surprise that the refrigerator was also full of her favorite mango yogurt, and she took out a carton and ate it, washing it down with the Tab.

When she'd finished her impromptu breakfast, she took another can of Tab and started toward the door, half expecting Mick or Alf to appear out of nowhere. She pushed against the jamb and the door slid open noiselessly. There was no way she could tell whether it had been locked during the night or not, and it was a waste of time to worry about it. There were some things you had to take on trust, and John was doped, bound and locked up in his habitat.

Of course, Libby was far from certain that John was the most dangerous creature on this island.

Fortunately she had always had a good sense of direction, since the long white-painted hallways had no distinguishing features. She made it down to the observation room without a single wrong turn, hoping against hope the place would be deserted.

No such luck. Alf and Mick were playing cards and drinking beer, and Mick raised his head as she appeared, an oddly sweet smile wreathing his villainous face. "Wondered if you were going to sleep all day," he said cheerfully. "Want a beer?"

She controlled her instinctive shudder, holding up her can of pop. "I've got my own."

"Poison," Alf growled. "That stuff's no good for you—it's all chemicals."

"But they taste delicious," she said serenely.

"Looks like the doc's in a better mood after a good night's sleep," Alf observed slyly. "You ready to deal with the ape-man?"

"John," she corrected him. And whether she liked it or not, Alf was right. After a good night's sleep she was far better able to deal with a bullying brute like him.

She glanced over at the screen. It was daylight, the sun filtering down through the heavy overgrowth, which answered her question as to how long she'd slept. John was still strapped to the gurney, comatose. "I thought you were going to lower his dosage."

"I did," Alf said, dealing the cards.

"He doesn't look any different. Any more alert."

Alf shrugged. "I only said I'd lower the dose slightly. As you rightly pointed out, it wouldn't do to get old Ed mad at me, and we can't afford to keep losing scientists. Someone might begin to wonder."

"Yeah, right," Libby muttered. Rest had put all her wild imaginings in perspective, showing Alf's dire warnings as the ridiculous melodrama that they were. Dr. McDonough had died in a car accident. It was tragic, but far from sinister, and if the half of what she'd heard about McDonough's nasty little peculiarities were true, it wasn't particularly tragic.

Nothing was going to happen to her. She'd do her job, make her observations and go back to Chicago to write the paper that would make her career.

Leaving John at the mercy of Alf and Ed Hunnicutt.

She wasn't going to think about that right now. "I'm going in to see him now," she said. "You can finish your game—I'll call you if I need you."

Alf shrugged. "Suit yourself, Doc. There's not much he can do, tied up like that. But you give a scream if it looks like he might break free."

"He can't break free, Alf," Mick said earnestly. "You've got him bound so tight you almost cut off the circulation in his hands..."

"Mick!" Alf said sharply. He gave Libby what he obviously hoped was a winning smile. "Mick exaggerates. He's got a soft heart for dumb creatures like himself."

Libby didn't smile back. "I want you to loosen his restraints. Enough so that he's comfortable."

"Oh, he's comfortable enough. He doesn't have any sense of what's going on, anyway. Those drugs keep him pretty well paralyzed."

"Then you don't need to restrain him so tightly."

Alf let out a long-suffering sigh. "Go and check the restraints, will you, Mick, before her ladyship has a hissy fit? I'll deal the next hand."

"Sure thing, Alf. How much am I down?"

"You're into me for your wages up until May, laddie," he cackled. "Maybe we'd be better off playing for matchsticks."

"You said it was no fun unless we played for money," Mick said.

Alf glared at him. "Go and check the restraints, Mick, and try not to think too hard."

Once again the heat and humidity of the habitat hit her as they stepped through the open door. The air was so thick she could hardly breathe, and even though the sun was filtered through the thick canopy of trees way overhead, she could still feel the heat beating down on her. In her case they wouldn't have had to drug or restrain her—just an hour or two in this liquid air and she'd be unable to move.

John was lying on the gurney, motionless, in the same position he'd been in twelve hours before when she'd left him. Mick busied himself with the hand restraints, loosening them a marginal amount. "I don't dare do any more, miss," he said apologetically. "At least this won't cut off the circulation. We don't want him able to slip his hands through, now, do we?"

"Of course not," she said absently. "You can go back to your game, Mick. I'll be a while."

"I don't know as I ought to leave you..."

"I'll be fine. You can hear and see me, and as Alf put it so charmingly, all I have to do is scream and you'll come running with the tranquilizer gun. Right?"

"Right," he said, still looking doubtful.

"Go along, Mick," she said gently. "I'll be fine."

She waited until the door closed behind him, closing them in together. In the daylight it was impossible to see beyond the fine mesh screen, but she had little doubt that Alf would manage to watch them and beat Mick at cards at the same time.

"How are you doing today, John?" she asked in a quiet voice, not much above a whisper. "Did they tie your wrists too tight? I thought I'd warned Alf, but I guess he doesn't learn. Are you still feeling as drugged as you were before?"

He didn't move, his eyelids didn't even flicker in his still, closed face. For some reason she'd been keeping her distance, but at his utter stillness she moved closer, staring at him in fascination. "You must hate it here," she murmured. "I don't blame you. Stolen away from your life in the wild, drugged and beaten. I don't believe you really killed Dr. McDonough, though I wouldn't be surprised if you'd wanted to. I think I would, too."

John didn't move. She came closer, so that she could keep her voice lower. She could hear Alf and Mick laughing as they played cards, and she felt a faint sense of relief. At least they wouldn't be staring at her, watching her every move, listening to her every word.

"I know how you feel," she murmured. The words wouldn't make sense, but the sooner he got used to the sound of her voice the better. "I feel trapped sometimes, and there's nothing I can do about it. In my case I chose my own trap, though. And most of the time it's perfectly fine. I like my job, my apartment, the city. It's very intellectually stimulating. Though I don't suppose you'd understand much about that kind of thing. I can go to the theater, to concerts, eat any kind of food I want. I don't really like to shop, but if I did I'd be able to find anything I wanted. It's really a good life for a single woman."

She took a deep breath and put her hands on him again. She'd brought a tape measure this time, and she carefully measured the length of his arms, his legs, his cranium, all without trying to jar him too much. "It would be a different matter if my parents were still alive," she continued. "But they're not, and since I was an only child I don't really have any ties. School became my family, and I've really been perfectly happy. I mean, where else could I go? Just take off? No, I belong in the city, even if it does feel like a straitjacket sometimes.

"I used to wish I'd been a normal sort of daughter, instead of some weird, intellectual freak. Maybe I'd be married now, have children, live in the suburbs. Though something tells me I wouldn't like the suburbs. At least in the city you can get a sense of privacy. Nobody pays any attention to you there."

She looked down into his still, beautiful face. "All I've done is spend the last ten years of my life in college. Why does anyone need two Ph.D.s and a master's degree? There's a limit to how much pleasure you can get out of being smarter than people twice your age. As a matter of fact, I think my pleasure in that ran out when I was about twenty. I'm almost thirty now, and the fact of the matter is, I'm sick of my life. Sometimes I think there's nothing I'd like better than to have some wild-game hunters carry me off to live in a rain forest. Depending, of course, on what they looked like," she added with a soft laugh.

She tilted his head slightly to look at the rope burns wreathed around his neck. They must have been horrible in the beginning. Now, almost three months later, the bruising was still vivid, and he was still only able to make growling sounds.

Though for all she knew, he'd never made any other kind of sound. "Your neck looks awful," she said under her breath. "Maybe I'm just as happy in my city apartment after all. I wouldn't want to be half strangled."

He had new bruises on his arm, and it was easy enough to guess what caused it. An overly enthusiastic jab of a hypodermic needle. If Alf had agreed to cut back in quantity, he'd obviously had to make up for it in delivery.

"He's a pig," she said softly. "I don't know how I'll get him to stop hurting you, but I promise I will. I need you to come out of that fog, to try to communicate with me. I know you don't want to trust me, but I'm the only one who can help you."

He didn't twitch, didn't blink, didn't move a muscle. Her soft words had fallen on deaf ears, and she started to pull back, defeated.

Not fast enough. His hand closed around her like a python's death grip, so hard that she felt her bones grind together. She stifled her moan of pain, but clearly not enough.

"What's going on in there?" Alf's voice came across the intercom.

It took all her effort to fight through the pain and sound calm. "Nothing, Mr. Droggan. I'm just talking to the subject."

"I told you, he can't understand you," Alf said. "Why don't you come on out here, grab and beer and join us in a friendly game of cards. I'll beat the pants off you."

"You wish," Libby said in a tight voice. She

stared down at the man lying on the gurney. His hand was wrapped around her wrist, so tightly that her hand was white beneath his grip. Apart from that he looked the same, his eyes closed, his breathing even.

"Let go of me," she whispered. "You're hurting me."

He didn't seem to have even heard her. She wondered whether he even knew what he was doing, or whether it was simply a reflex, but she wasn't sure she cared. It hurt unbearably, enough so that she was shaking, and she didn't know how to stop him.

"Please," she whispered in a trembling voice. "You're going to break my wrist. I don't mean you any harm, but if the men find out they'll come in here and hurt you. I don't want that to happen. Please, let go of me."

He didn't respond, and the grip on her wrist was like fire. Her hand was going numb, but not a nice, pain-free numb. A burning, agonizing numbness.

It would be useless to try to pry his long fingers off her wrist, and she didn't even bother to try. Instead she put her other hand over his manacle-like grip, trying to soothe him with long, gentle strokes. "Please," she whispered again, and her voice broke. "It hurts."

She was beyond thinking, she was just trying to concentrate on controlling the pain, when he released her, so suddenly that she fell backward, onto the ground, faint with pain.

"What's up in there?" Alf's voice thundered over the speaker.

"Tripped," she said breathlessly, cradling her arm against her stomach. "Tripped over my own clumsy feet," she said in a stronger voice, scrambling to stand up again. She felt light-headed, dizzy from the pain. She looked down, and the red marks around her wrist were a suitable match to the marks around John's neck. She flexed her hand cautiously, wiggling her fingers, but everything moved easily.

She glanced up at him, but he lay there like a monolith. Maybe he hadn't even known what he was doing with that fierce, painful grip. Except that if he hadn't known, he could have easily broken her wrist, she knew that now. His strength was phenomenal, even with it blunted by tranquilizers, and he could have snapped her wrist with no effort at all.

He hadn't. And he'd released her. She didn't dare get too close to him, but it seemed as if his breathing was marginally faster. His face was immobile, and there was no way she could tell if he had even the faintest trace of consciousness. She wasn't going to get close enough to find out.

"Don't do that again," she whispered. "I told you I'd help you, and I will. But you have to promise not to hurt me."

Who was she kidding? He didn't understand a word she was saying, much less concepts like promise or even hurt. And how could she help him if he continued to present a danger?

And for that matter, when and why had she decided to help him? It was the damned weakness of hers, humanizing the data. But this data was human, a living, breathing man kept captive by a billionaire and a sweet fool and a sadist. And she was the only one who could help him.

She just wasn't sure why she should try.

"You all right, miss?" Mick looked up from his card game as she reentered the observation room.

"Just fine," she said, keeping her bruised wrist out of sight. "I'm going back to my room to read over some of Professor McDonough's notes. I'll be back later."

"Not too much later, Doc," Alf said. "I kept the place open for you last night as a special favor, but from now on it's lights out for Tarzan by 6:00 p.m. Mick and I need a life, too."

She didn't bother arguing with him. If they abandoned the observation room early then it would give her more of a chance to see John without an audience. To see whether he was really as unconscious as he appeared to be. To see whether she could find some way to communicate with him without Alf watching and listening.

To see if she could find any answers to the thousand-and-one questions that plagued her. Who was he? What was he doing on a remote island off Australia?

And why had she decided to help him?

Chapter Five

The first thing Libby did when she got back to her room was empty out a tray of ice cubes onto a hand towel and wrap it around her wrist. The marks of his long, strong fingers stood out, dark against her pale flesh, troubling. Had it been a reflex on his part? Had he wanted to hurt her as he'd hurt Alf? For what reason?

There she went again, identifying with the data. Richard would be totally disgusted with her. Which, in fact, was a good thing, since she was totally disgusted with Richard and with the fact that she'd ever considered him attractive. Well, he had been attractive, she admitted to herself, in a bland, civilized way.

She froze in horror. Why was she suddenly considering "civilized" to be a detriment? One day in the presence of a wild man and she was starting to alter her idea of what was attractive? In a week she might even start thinking that she wasn't made for city life, when she knew perfectly well she was. She loved the city, the noise, the bustle, the excitement. She could never live anywhere else, certainly not in the wilderness—

"Stop it," she said out loud, the sound of her voice startling in the stillness. "It's jet lag."

Jet lag. And the still figure of a man, a savage, trapped like a beautiful wild animal, caged and drugged and destroyed.

She kicked off her shoes and lay back on the bed. It was actually a better mattress than the one she owned in Chicago—she'd been meaning to replace hers. Obviously Edward J. Hunnicutt wanted the best for his minions.

Minions. Was she a minion as well? She certainly never thought that was her goal in life. And yet here she was, at the back end of beyond where she wasn't even sure what country they were in, at the beck and call of a billionaire, doing something she wasn't even sure she wanted to be doing. For the sake of grant money and career. For some reason, she wasn't sure if it was a price she was willing to pay.

She needed to see John without anyone around, watching. To see whether he could communicate with her. It would be safe enough—she'd just be certain not to get within reach. Even trussed up and drugged he'd managed to do a certain amount of damage to her wrist. But if she kept her distance, watched out for those strong hands of his, she'd be fine.

She needed him to open his eyes. It was that simple. If she could look into his eyes she'd be able to tell whether he'd be able to communicate. Whether he was a man or an animal.

She ought to set the alarm clock. She didn't want another night to go by without finding out what lay behind the dark, impassive face of the creature tied to the gurney. But she was too tired to move. Just a moment's rest, she thought, and then she'd get up, find something to eat, set the alarm. Just a few minutes more…

She woke up in a pool of water. The ice had melted, soaking her clothes, dripping on the bed beneath her. The climate of the room was controlled so perfectly she hadn't even realized she'd been soaking wet, and she moaned as she climbed out of bed.

The lights went from dim to bright, and she glanced at the clock. Five-thirty. It had to be morning, not afternoon—she couldn't have slept the clock around. She wouldn't be so wet if twenty-four hours had passed.

She stripped off the damp clothes and dumped them on the bathroom floor. She pulled on a pair of shorts and a T-shirt, shoved her feet in sandals and opened the door into the hallway.

The observation room was dark. The door opened automatically for her, a relief when she'd half expected it to be locked. The lights came up to half-wattage, probably on some sort of timer, and she walked to the screen, staring intently into the habitat.

She couldn't see anything in the darkness. She couldn't tell whether the sun had risen yet or not, but if it had it hadn't managed to penetrate the thick growth that surrounded the area. She couldn't see anything, and she had no idea how to control the lights other than walk in there and trigger the automatic sensor.

The door to the habitat wasn't locked, either. Obviously Alf was much too trusting. Not that he'd have any right to forbid her—after all, she was here to observe the subject, and scientific observation should come first.

But she somehow suspected that Alf wasn't going to see it that way.

She stepped into the darkness, and the door slid shut behind her. Unfortunately the lights didn't come on, and she had to make do with the dim glow from beyond the one-way screen and the faint light of dawn filtering down through the towering trees overhead.

She headed in the direction of the gurney, moving carefully, trusting her instincts. She didn't want to make the mistake of bumping into it, giving him a chance to grab her again with that manacle-like grip. She'd managed to get him to release her before, but there was no guarantee she could do so again. Besides, if he grabbed her already-bruised wrist she'd probably scream loud enough to wake Alf and Mick, and that was the last thing she wanted.

She took a cautious step forward, her eyes slowly growing accustomed to the dimness. She could make out the shape of the gurney in the shadows, and she moved toward it, then stopped in shock.

The gurney was empty.

She looked up, out over the vast expanse and into the barely glimmering darkness, and her skin prickled. Something, someone was watching her.

She tried to calm herself. It wasn't necessarily John, she reminded herself. Alf and Mick might put him somewhere else for the night, and the top of the habitat was open to the sky. Birds could swoop in and nest, and probably other creatures could climb whatever fenced the place in, or burrow under the electric wire. It was probably something utterly harmless, staring at her out of the darkness. Like a raccoon, or the Australian equivalent of a raccoon. She had absolutely nothing to worry about. She just had to get her butt out of there as quickly as she could.

The one thing she wasn't going to do was run. Years ago, when she'd been a child, she'd been visiting her grandmother's farm in Vermont, and she'd gone for a walk in an adjoining field, only to come face-to-face with about twenty baby cows. The heifers had stared at her curiously, and she'd stared back. And then she'd started to back up, away from them.

To her horror they'd moved forward, curious. She walked a little faster, the fence in the distance. They speeded up as well. Suddenly she'd panicked, turning and running to the gate and vaulting over it as the herd of cows stampeded after her, their hooves thundering on the ground.

She'd been sitting in the dirt, crying, when her grandmother had come out. She'd taken one look at Libby with her grazed knees and dirty, tear-streaked face, walked over to the fence where the heifers were crowded, and said in a loud, commanding voice, "Shoo!"

And they'd scattered, running off in fear for their life.

They never stopped teasing Libby about her terror of the harmless heifers. Probably one reason why she cherished the city. At least there all the wild animals were on two legs.

And so was the wild animal she'd come in search of, she reminded herself grimly. And her still-sore wrist was proof that he was a great deal more dangerous than a herd of curious heifers.

She took a step backward, then another, unable

to shake the memory of the cows. It had been when she'd turned her back and run that they'd broken free, charging after her. As long as she stayed calm, in control, then she'd be safe. Show fear, and she was toast.

The ground was rough beneath her feet, but she didn't waste her time glancing down. It would be too dark to see, and she didn't want to distract herself. She let her feet slide lightly across the dirt, so that she wouldn't accidentally trip on something, trying to be calm. She hadn't made the mistake of saying anything—he might not even know she was trapped in there with him, defenseless, unprotected.

She was almost at the door. A faint glow filtered through the screen, and the sky overhead was growing paler in the morning light. Just a few more feet, she thought. Surely she could turn and run now. He wouldn't be able to catch her in that short distance. If he was even inside the habitat, if he was even aware that she'd been incredibly stupid enough to have stepped inside it without making sure he was strapped down.

Another foot, and she could turn and run. Just one more, and she'd be safe. One more.

She spun around, ready to sprint to the door, and slammed up against him.

She let out a muffled shriek of terror, one she tried to stifle, though she wasn't sure why. He seemed absolutely huge, looming over her in the darkness, and she'd never felt so small and fragile in her entire life.

He didn't touch her. He didn't need to—his very proximity was threat enough. His eyes were open, but they were dark, dilated by the drugs and the darkness, and she couldn't see anything but dark black holes of blank rage.

"Don't hurt me," she whispered. "Please."

He didn't even blink, staring down at her with a kind of dazed intensity. She was acutely conscious of everything, of the vast amounts of smooth, warm flesh in front of her, of the sky lightening overhead, the sound of the birds, the smell of tropical flowers and plants. Not a bad memory for the last one in her life, she thought in a kind of stupor, half prepared for one of his huge hands to come down on her, crushing her into oblivion.

He still didn't move. And then a raw, rasping sound came from deep inside of him, painful, tortured, more an expelling of breath than words.

She stared up at him, confusion obliterating her panic. "I don't understand. What are you saying?"

He made the noise again, harsh, guttural, incomprehensible, and for some crazy reason she reached toward him, wanting to touch him, wanting to calm him.

The lights came on full force, startling them both. And then a moment later he'd disappeared into the thick undergrowth, seconds before the door slid open, exposing a fully armed Alf and Mick.

"What the hell are you doing in there, Doc?" Alf demanded. "You want to get yourself killed?"

It took all her strength of will to appear calm and unruffled. "Where's our subject?" she asked innocently. "I couldn't sleep, so I thought I'd come down and observe him, but he's not on the gurney and I haven't seen him anywhere."

"Good thing for it," Alf said. "He could snap your neck like it was a bunch of twigs. What kind of fool are you to walk in there with him running loose?"

"I had no idea he was running loose—it was too dark to see the gurney. And you'd led me to believe you kept him drugged and tied up twenty-four seven."

"We could hardly do that, miss," Mick piped up, his face worried. "He's got to be free to roam, to take care of business, if you know what I mean."

"No," she said, confused.

"He means he's not going to be giving him a bath or changing his diapers and neither am I," Alf said with a snort. "We undo his bonds and keep his dosage low so he can move around during the night."

"And how do you get him trussed up again in the morning?"

The smile in Alf's deceptively pleasant face was

chilling. "We do a bit of hunting," he said, patting the rifle he was carrying with affection. "God knows it's boring enough here—we need a little sport to help us pass the time. Mick can't hit the broadside of a barn with one of these, but I've gotten quite good at it."

"Hey, I can use a handgun," Mick protested.

Alf frowned at him. "I don't think the lady doc needs to know that. Are you coming out, miss, or are you just going to stand there waiting for Tarzan to swoop down on a vine and carry you off? Maybe that's what you've got in mind, eh?"

"Don't be disgusting, Mr. Droggan," she said briskly, moving past him. "And I don't want you shooting him with your tranquilizer darts today. Let him move around the place freely."

"No can do, miss. I've got orders from Hunnicutt, and he's the one who pays the bills. We need to get readings on him, take some blood—"

"Take some blood!" she repeated in shock. "How much do you take?"

"Only about four ounces. Not enough to matter."

"Every day? You'll kill him!"

"Did he look dead? I don't think it even slows him down. And his blood is like liquid gold—the market's enormous."

"Why? Why would anyone want his blood?"

"It's pure. Untainted by civilization. Drug companies and research and development departments have a thirst like a vampire for the stuff. We started out taking half a pint every day but he began to look a bit pale, so Old Ed had us cut back. At least until we can get him to eat meat and liver. Right now he's strictly veggie.''

''But what about the drugs?''

''They can filter 'em out, no problem. They're the newest thing in tranquilizers. Bloody miracle drugs, they are.''

''Leave him alone, Mr. Droggan,'' she said, unable to keep a faint, pleading note out of her voice.

It did no good, of course. ''No, Dr. Holden,'' he said flatly. ''I've got my orders. If you've got a problem with anything take it up with Old Ed. He'll probably be back tomorrow or the next day to see how things are going. He never stays away long— Tarzan's his newest toy on Christmas morning, and he's going to play with it until he breaks it.''

''That's what I'm afraid of,'' Libby said in a quiet voice. She still hadn't moved. Mick and Alf were on one side of the sliding door, she was on the other, still in the steaming atmosphere of the habitat. Where had John disappeared to? He must have known Mick and Alf would come armed, but why hadn't he hurt her? What had he been trying to say to her? If, indeed, he was actually trying to communicate. It might have been just wishful thinking on her part.

Mick stuck his gun inside the door, peering into the murky darkness. "You sure he's not around, miss? You wouldn't want him jumping out at you from the bush. He's a wild animal."

"He's not..."

"I've had enough," Alf said flatly, stepping over the doorstep, gun at the ready. "Now, get your pretty little arse out of here or I'll be using the dart gun on you, missy."

"You wouldn't dare," she said. But the problem was, she knew he would. Somewhere in the darkness John was watching, listening. Not understanding, of course, if she could go by the blankness of his expression.

"You're a cheap bully, Mr. Droggan," she said sharply, moving toward the door.

"No, miss. I'm a very expensive bully. Ain't I, Mick?" Alf rumbled with laughter at his own humor.

She couldn't look back. The door slid shut behind her, closing the two men in with their guns and their prey, and there was nothing she could do to stop them, nothing at all. For some reason she wanted to cry, and she wasn't sure if she could keep blaming jet lag.

Her bed was only slightly damp from the melted ice, and she flung herself down on it, anyway, cradling her wrist. It didn't hurt as much as it had, though it was definitely bruised, the marks of his fingers purple and blue against her pale skin. For some reason she had the absurd fancy that he'd hate it if he knew that he'd hurt her. Ridiculous. How could he not know?

What had he said in that rasping, ruined voice? Had he used actual words? Did he even know words? What was he trying so desperately to tell her?

He hadn't touched her, when he could have so easily. Hadn't hurt her, had simply disappeared when the door opened, though animal instinct must have told him that if he took hold of her he'd have something they wanted.

Of course, he might have known they'd simply hurt him even more. Knowing Alf, he probably would have shot her first, then taken aim on John. What was that line in the movie *Speed?* ''Shoot the hostage''? Alf would have taken great pleasure in shooting her.

What had he been trying to tell her? The sounds, the look on his face swirled around and around in her mind, but no matter how hard she tried to force it, it wouldn't come into focus.

Had the harsh rasp of his voice come from the damage the hunters had inflicted on his neck? Or had he lived alone in the jungle, never using his voice, so that when he tried it came out like the pained cry of an animal? Was there any way she was going to find out?

She couldn't stand this. To hell with Edward J. Hunnicutt's bottomless pockets, to hell with her career, to hell with everything. Richard used to tell her she didn't have the killer instinct, and until she developed it she wouldn't reach the top level in her field.

If she had to be ruthless, then maybe the prize wasn't worth the price. Besides, what did she really want in life? The chance to do research, to study in peace. She hated academic politics, hated the stupid games she had to play with people to keep them from interfering.

She wasn't going to let them do this to John. Not going to let them bleed him, day after day, until he was so weakened he could hardly move. Not let them hunt him nightly, for a twisted kind of sport. Not let them use him like a circus freak for the gratification of Hunnicutt's ego.

And suddenly something in her brain clicked, and she knew what he'd said. Those harsh, guttural sounds, almost unrecognizable, before he'd disappeared back in the dense foliage.

"Help me," he'd said. She was sure of it.

And she was going to do exactly that. She was going to set him free.

Chapter Six

When Libby walked back into the observation room late that afternoon Mick and Alf were playing cards again. Alf was probably cheating, from the expression on Mick's sorrowful face, and neither of them bothered to do more than give her a cursory glance when she opened the door.

"Did you catch him?" she asked in a deceptively even tone of voice. The very thought of hunting him through that tangled jungle made her sick to her stomach, but any more protests would be a waste of time.

"'Course we did," Alf said, taking a leisurely sip of beer before discarding. "Got him in the left shoulder. He went down like a log. So don't give me trouble about any fresh bruises. He got them falling."

"But Alf, you forgot you—"

"Shut up, Mick," Alf said pleasantly.

Mick shut up, glancing uneasily over his cards at Libby. "Want to play a hand, Doc? Alf's a real master at cards."

"No, thanks. I wanted to read some of Dr. McDonough's research. The stuff in my room is incomplete."

Alf lay down his cards to look at her. "And what might you be wanting to know?"

Libby shrugged, trying to look no more than casually interested. "Oh, normal stuff. Weight, blood pressure, reaction to stimuli. Mick said McDonough thought he might be deaf until he tested him. I'd like to see the results of those tests, among other things."

Alf was still looking suspicious, but the beer and the poker were clearly higher priorities. "Left-hand filing drawer. There are CD-ROMs there with the information. McDonough ran the gamut."

"He even tried electroshock," Mick offered. "You should have seen Tarzan...er, John, jerk. You'd think he was flat-out cold, Dr. McDonough would apply the electrodes and wham! He'd jump a mile."

"I don't think Dr. Holden is interested in hearing about that," Alf said, frowning. "She's got a tender heart, you know. She's worried we're going to hurt the creature. She doesn't realize that he's like an animal. He doesn't hurt easily, and the moment it's over he's forgotten it."

"And how would you be knowing that, Mr. Droggan?" Libby asked, flipping through the CDs. "Did he tell you so?"

"You know as well as I do that he can't communicate. His brain hasn't evolved to that level. He's a throwback, more animal than human...."

"I appreciate the benefit of your scientific observations, Mr. Droggan. But he might very well be suffering from brain damage. When someone is nearly strangled it cuts off oxygen to the brain. He may have been verbal and intelligent before Hunnicutt decided to send a crew of thugs to capture him."

"We weren't the ones who captured him!" Mick protested.

"We're not the thugs she means, laddie," Alf said with a snort. "We're not responsible for the shape he was in when he got here."

"But you're responsible for the shape he's in now," she muttered.

As expected, Alf had grown tired of her criticism. "We're trying to concentrate on our game, missy. Do you mind?"

"Not at all," she said, humming noisily under her breath as she opened drawers, keeping her body between the two men and what she was looking for.

The drugs were easy enough to find. A dozen doses of the tranquilizer, prepackaged with syringes attached, plus another twenty-four tranquilizer darts. She ran the water in the sink, to cover the sound of her activities, but Alf didn't even bother to look up.

Easy enough to squirt the drugs into the sink and refill the syringe with tap water. The seal on each dose was broken, but she was taking a chance Alf wouldn't notice. She was almost finished, ready to start on the tranquilizer darts, when Alf's voice startled her.

"Bring us a beer, love," he said. "Since you're already over there you can prove yourself useful."

If Libby had had any qualms about what she intended to do they vanished instantly.

"Certainly," she said sweetly, opening the refrigerator and pulling out two dark bottles of Guinness. She would have made an excellent spy, she thought smugly. She opened the bottles and squirted two of the remaining syringes into each one before she turned around, and neither Mick nor Alf even noticed the delay.

"That's a good lass," Alf said dryly when she presented him with the bottle. "If this science thing doesn't work out you can always be a barmaid."

She gave him a sour smile before turning back to the sink, busily covering up any sign of what she'd been doing. She pulled a few CDs at random, then turned back to the men. "What time are you shutting this place down?"

Alf yawned noisily. He'd already drained half the

bottle of Guinness, and she realized he had six empty ones on the floor near him already, with Mick keeping pace. Maybe she hadn't needed to put the drugs in the beer after all—they'd probably drunk enough to pass out.

Then again, better safe than sorry. Beer and tranquilizers wouldn't kill them—they were too mean.

"What's it to you?" Alf demanded belligerently.

"I'm here to do a job. I need to know when I can do it."

"If you hadn't slept all day you would have had plenty of time," he replied. "We're shutting down early, so you'll just have to entertain yourself with reading Dr. McDonough's research. Pretty dry stuff if you ask me. Mick, go in and unfasten the restraints on Tarzan."

Mick looked startled. "Are you sure? We cut back on the stuff today because we thought Dr. Holden would be working with him...."

"We didn't cut back that much, old son. If you're too chicken to go in there then I'll take care of it," Alf said, rising on slightly unsteady feet. Had he been drunk before and she just hadn't realized it, Libby thought. Or had the drugs already taken effect?

"I'll do it," Mick said reluctantly. "You want to watch my back in case he's livelier than we expect?"

That was the last thing Libby wanted. Alf would

use any excuse to shoot John, and she needed him as alert as possible if she was going to help him.

"I'll come with you," she offered hastily. "The tranquilizer gun's pretty straightforward, isn't it? Point and shoot?"

"Ever used a gun before, little lady?" Alf said, mocking her.

"Skeet shooting champion three years in a row," she said, a barefaced lie. She'd never touched a gun in her thirty years and would have happily spent the next thirty without that experience.

"All right," Mick said. He was sounding a little out of it as well, and his drugged bottle was half empty, too. He went over to a tall closet, pulled out a rifle and handed it to her. "Simple as pie. Just don't get excited and shoot me in the bum by accident."

"I wouldn't think of it," she said. If she'd had any experience with guns that probably would have been an easier task. She could have just shot Mick and Alf with the drugs, instead of trying to sneak it into them. At least it appeared to be working.

She stood in the doorway, the cold steel of the gun cradled in her arms, watching as Mick made his unsteady way toward the gurney. John was lying there, motionless, and she held her breath, half afraid he might be conscious enough to grab at Mick.

But he lay still as Mick fumbled with the wrist

and leg restraints. "Sleeping Beauty," Mick muttered beneath his breath, eyeing John warily.

He took the gun from her as the door closed, putting it back in the closet. It took him two tries to open it. Alf was already standing by the door, weaving. His bottle of beer was now empty.

"I'm going to bed," Alf said. "Been a long day."

"So it has," Mick agreed, squinting at his watch. He moved it closer to his eyes, then farther away, clearly unable to get it into focus. He gave up, giving Libby a sweetly loopy smile. "Come along, Doc. Dangerous things in here."

Alf had already shuffled off down the corridor, safely forgetting her existence. Libby grabbed a handful of CD-ROMs and followed after them. The moment she stepped through the doorway the lights in the observation room automatically dimmed, and the door slid shut behind them.

"Better lock the door, Mick," Alf called over his shoulder. "Don't want the doc making another mistake and wandering where she shouldn't."

"I don't know how, Alfie," Mick said plaintively, but Alf just kept going, walking with a faintly rolling gait like a sailor who'd just made landfall.

Mick turned and looked at her owlishly. "You won't do anything you shouldn't?"

"Wouldn't think of it," she said cheerfully. "Where do you guys sleep?"

"Down one level."

"You thinkin' of visiting?" Alf rumbled from far away. Obviously he wasn't that drugged yet.

"In your dreams, Mr. Droggan," she said flatly.

His chuckle drifted back. "Been there. Done that."

He disappeared down a flight of stairs at the end of the hall, and Libby waited until Mick had followed after him. She didn't want to wait too long—there still might be some daylight left if she got John out now.

If only she didn't feel so guilty about drugging Mick and Alf. Well, not that Alf made her feel particularly guilty, but she wasn't quite sure what kind of dosage she'd given them. Something strong enough to halt a prime specimen like John might be a bit much for two couch potatoes like Mick and Alf.

She waited, holding her breath. And then she heard a loud crash.

"Damn," she muttered, racing down the hall after them, skittering down the stairs to the lower level. The hallway looked identical to the one above it, to all the hallways in this strange compound. Except for Mick's figure sprawled on the floor outside the open door.

She knelt down beside him, feeling for a pulse,

so desperate that she almost missed it at first. There was a loud, growling noise from the room beyond, and she looked up to see Alf spread-eagled across a bed, snoring loudly.

A moment later she found Mick's pulse, slow and strong, and she almost wept with relief. "Mick," she said, shaking his shoulder.

He made a "mmff" noise, not even opening his eyes. She tried again, but he had passed out.

She couldn't just leave him there. If it had been Alf it would have been a different matter, but obviously Alf's bigger build had enabled him to get farther before the drugs had kicked in. She put her arms under Mick's and began to drag him into the room.

For such a slight man he weighed a hell of a lot, though it was probably because he was a dead weight. She got him halfway into the room and had to give up, exhausted. He lay on the floor, a peaceful smile on his face, and she was tempted to get him a pillow and a blanket, then decided against it.

She was hoping against hope that they'd simply figure they'd had too much to drink, that they wouldn't realize she'd helped them along. Of course, that was probably ridiculous on her part. After all, when they woke up, John would be gone, and at least Alf had the brains to figure out he couldn't have done it on his own.

She could come up with some sort of convincing

story if she put her mind to it, she supposed. Something about John escaping when she opened the door to check on him. Alf wouldn't believe her, but what could he do about it?

Her career would be in tatters, of course. Edward J. Hunnicutt was not the sort of patron you crossed. At this point she really didn't care. She wasn't going to let them play their torturous games with John anymore. She didn't care how high a price she had to pay.

The door closed quietly behind her when she stepped back into the hall, and the conjoined snores of Hunnicutt's minions were almost inaudible. She took a deep breath, then started back down the hall. She had to work fast.

She'd already dressed wisely, in loose khaki cargo pants, a T-shirt and sandals. She needed to be able to move, and move fast, with an unpredictable force like John. She could only hope he was conscious enough to walk out of there.

The door to the observation room slid open, the lights set on half power, and she almost went straight to the habitat, thinking better of it at the last minute. "It's not that I don't trust you, John," she said out loud, grateful for the sound of her voice breaking the ominous stillness, "but a girl can never be too careful." She took a small handful of the remaining tranquilizer darts and shoved them in her pocket before heading for the habitat.

The door slid open as she neared it, a little too quickly for her peace of mind, and she hesitated, afraid to take that final step. "I must be out of my mind," she said in a voice so low no one else could hear it. Not that it mattered—there was no one there who could understand anything she said. "I'm destroying everything I spent my life working for. I'll never get a job in academia again—I'll be lucky if I find a job flipping hamburgers. Then again, that's probably not even an issue since John will probably break my neck."

There was an answer from the jungle beyond that portal. The mocking call of some bird, laughing at her predicament. "Typical," she muttered. "But I'm not turning back now."

She was about to step over the portal when she remembered the damned door didn't open automatically from the inside. Not when the wild man was roaming free. Grabbing a chair, she blocked the doorway with it, keeping it open, as she stepped into the steaming heat of the habitat.

He still lay on the gurney, unmoving, even though his fetters had been loosened, and she knew a moment's panic. What if they'd shot him so full of dope that he wouldn't be able to move until Alf and Mick started coming around? Was she destroying her career for nothing?

Not for nothing. Her father had spent his life in the service of others, helping wherever he could.

He taught her the price and the glory of idealism, of doing what you think is right no matter what the cost. She'd let him down before by retreating into her academic ivory tower; she wouldn't let him down again. She was doing this in memory of her father and all the people he'd helped. So all she was helping was a savage who could neither talk nor understand, who might very well be so damaged from his capture that he'd never be able to live free again. It was worth the risk.

"John?" Her voice wobbled slightly in the darkness. He didn't stir, not even a muscle, and she had no choice but to move closer, within reach. He hadn't grabbed her the last time, when he'd loomed over her in the darkness. There was no reason why he'd hurt her now.

Except that she had no guarantee that reason comprised any part of his makeup. And she'd come too far to turn back now.

She came up to the gurney and made herself touch his shoulder. Smooth, warm flesh, resilient and strong. "John," she said in a low voice. "I'm going to get you out of here."

The only thing that moved were his eyelids. His eyes opened at the sound of her voice, and he stared up at her. She had no idea whether he had any idea what she was saying, but she kept on, hoping some part would penetrate.

"I'm going to help you get away. That's what

you were saying this morning, wasn't it? You said 'help me,' didn't you? And I'm going to. I'm not going to let them drain your blood or hunt you with guns or use electric shock on you. You're going to be free again.''

He didn't move, his expression the same, uncomprehending blank. His eyes were dark in his face, and he stared at her, soundless. Mindless?

She took his hand in hers, remembering the strength in his long fingers, determined not to show fear. ''Come.'' She tugged at him.

He sat up on the gurney, slowly, looking around him. She took a step away, waiting for him to climb down off the stretcher, but he didn't move. Just stared at her.

''Come on, John,'' she said. ''Come on.'' She slapped her thigh in a beckoning motion, and then laughed. ''God, I'm treating you like a dog. 'Here, Lassie, come on, girl,''' she mocked herself.

He didn't even blink.

''Please, John,'' she said, not bothering to disguise the pleading note in her voice. There was always the possibility that he understood a language other than English. If so, he'd at least recognize the need in her voice. ''I'm not even sure of the way out of here, and the sooner I get you going the safer you'll be. Please?'' She held out her hand to him, trying to ignore the fact that it trembled.

She didn't know whether he'd understood her or

was just ready to move. He slid off the gurney, and there was no drugged slowness to his movement. He didn't take her hand, but he waited, as if expecting her to lead the way.

"Good," she said, nodding. "Come with me." She went to the door, pushing the chair out of the way, standing in the portal, waiting for him.

The few moments he waited seemed almost endless. And then he moved, crossing the expanse of phony jungle habitat, moving past her in the doorway, his body brushing against her.

And he was free.

Chapter Seven

She led the way down the long, white corridors, up the narrow flights of stairs, with John moving silently behind her, so silently that she twice glanced back to make certain he was still there. That he hadn't wandered off in a drugged daze. She needed to get him out of the house, into the relative freedom of the uninhabited island before Mick and Alf regained consciousness. She wasn't really sure what she was going to do beyond that.

By the time she reached the pristine front entrance of Edward J. Hunnicutt's jungle fortress her heart was racing. For some reason John's presence behind her, looming over her, didn't frighten her the way it should have. He was little more than a wild animal, she still bore the marks from when he'd practically crushed her wrist, and Alf's cast was impressive indeed. Not to mention the nasty rumors of Dr. McDonough's untimely demise. Had

John been responsible for that? And given the fact that McDonough had tormented him with electric shock and God knows what else, could she really blame him?

It wasn't up to her to pass judgment. She needed to free him, it was that simple. Once she let him out of the compound he was no longer her responsibility. She would have followed her conscience, done what she knew was right. It was up to John and his lifetime of surviving in the jungle to take care of the rest.

She half expected the front door to come equipped with some kind of security system. No alarms would wake Mick and Alf from their drugged stupor, so she wasn't worried, but to her surprise the door slid open without hesitation when she approached it. Obviously Hunnicutt had great faith in the remoteness of Ghost Island.

It was growing dark, the sky overheard was a deep indigo, and she blinked, trying to become accustomed to it. She'd never had particularly good night vision, and this remote island made it even worse, with no ambient streetlights to help her focus.

John had come up beside her, and he stared out into the gathering night. "There it is," she said. "Freedom. Mick and Alf won't come to for hours now—you should be able to just disappear into the jungle. Someone will probably come after you again, but at least this time you'll know they're coming. You'll have a fighting chance. I wish there was something more I could do to help you, but I'm a city girl. You're on your own out there.''

He stepped through the door, then turned back to look at her. It took her a moment to realize he was waiting for her to follow him.

She laughed lightly, nervously, shaking her head. ''No, I'm not coming with you. You're going alone. I'd just get in the way, and besides, I'm not made for jungle life. You'd better go now. You don't want to waste even a moment of time.''

He didn't move, didn't respond, just waited for her. Then he held out his hand to her.

There was no denying he had beautiful hands. Long, well-shaped fingers, like an artist's. Not the clublike hands of a savage. No denying that when he disappeared into the jungle an odd, dreamlike part of her life would disappear with him.

She shook her head again, the only way she knew how to communicate with him. ''No,'' she said. ''I'm staying here.''

He simply took a step forward, caught her hand in his iron grip and yanked her forward, across the threshold, into the dense tropical evening, and began dragging her along after him.

She'd forgotten how strong he was. And how damnably impervious to anything she might say. All her protests fell on uncomprehending ears, all her struggles were useless. He dragged her after him, into the jungle, and there was nothing she could do to stop his inexorable advance. She tripped and fell, but he simply hauled her up again and continued onward, and she stumbled after him, trying to control her panic.

The night was alive around them, the tropical birds screeching overhead, the air so thick and humid it was practically breathing. The thick growth brushed against her, but John moved ahead like a stalking panther, seemingly unaware of his unwilling partner. She wondered if she could bite him, but he was moving so fast, keeping her at arm's length behind him, that she would have had to scamper to catch up enough to sink her teeth into him, and the logistics didn't seem possible. Sooner or later he'd slow down, sooner or later he'd have to loosen his grip, and then she'd run.

They were moving deeper and deeper into the tropical growth, and she was having a hard time catching her breath, both because of the pace and the density of the thick, humid air. "You really...ought to...let me go," she panted. "I'll just slow you down. I can't...imagine why you'd want to take me...with you."

It was harder to keep up with him while she was trying to argue, and since he was paying absolutely no attention it was undoubtedly a waste of what little energy she had left. However, if she dropped from exhaustion he'd have to leave her, and the sooner the better. They were already so deep in the jungle she was going to have a hell of a time finding her way back to the compound. She might have to count on Mick and Alf coming out with a search party, and it wouldn't be her they were looking for.

She tripped again, going down hard, and he turned around and stared at her, his eyes black as midnight in the twilight forest. And then, before she realized what he was doing, he reached down and pulled her up, tossing her over his shoulder like a sack of potatoes.

"What the hell do you think you're doing? Put me down! Drop me, damn it!" She fought like crazy, kicking, pounding his back as he continued to move deeper into the jungle, seemingly oblivious to her struggles. His shoulder was hard beneath her stomach, but punching the smooth, muscled skin of his back wasn't having any effect apart from unsettling her, so she tried to wiggle, kicking at him.

To her utter astonishment he smacked her butt, hard, never slowing his rapid stride through the undergrowth. She was so startled she stopped struggling. Her panic began to recede, as it was replaced with a slow-burning, fiery hot rage that made her speechless. It was no loss—he couldn't understand a damned word she said, but the moment he put her down she was going to blister him with every insult she could think of. And then she'd kick him in the balls.

It had always looked so romantic in those old pirate movies, where some dashing Hollywood hero would carry the heroine off over his shoulder like a trophy. In truth, it was damned uncomfortable. Each smooth step jarred her stomach, and she wondered what he'd do if she threw up down his back? Probably wouldn't even notice.

And besides, she wasn't nauseous, but uncomfortable. She was trapped with a savage, being dragged off into the jungle, and for what? No good deed goes unpunished, Richard always used to say. This time he was proved right. Unless it was punishment for drugging Alf and Mick.

If so, it was a little extreme. She'd only done to them what they'd been doing to John, in spades. Surely fate wouldn't condemn her for an act meant only to help?

Fate didn't seem the slightest bit disposed toward her at the moment, as she went bouncing along through the ever-thickening forest, tossed over the wild man's shoulder like a sack of potatoes. The forest seemed endless as they traveled deeper, deeper into the jungle. The night grew black around her and she couldn't even see the trees that surrounded them. It was just as well John was carrying her. She wouldn't have been able to find her own way—she'd probably walk smack into a tree if she had to rely on her own two feet.

She lost track of time. When he finally halted it was pitch-black, and when he slid her off his shoulder to stand in front of him she could feel her knees shaking, and she almost collapsed before his hands clamped around her arms, supporting her.

"Are you going to let me go?" she demanded. At this point she couldn't even be certain she wanted him to release her—they were in the middle of absolutely nowhere and the night was pitch-black around them. She thought she could hear wild animals rustling in the undergrowth, and she had no idea what sort of creature she might run up against if she tried to find her way back to the compound on her own. Chances were they'd be more deadly than the man towering over her. Though there were no guarantees.

He pushed her down on the ground, quite gently, and then released her, stepping away. "God, I wish I could communicate with you!" she said, exasperated. "If I had even the faintest idea what goes on behind that blank expression of yours it would make my life a hell of a lot easier. Where are you going?"

But he vanished into the darkness before he could answer. Not that he would, of course. He couldn't speak. Or could he?

And how long should she stay sitting here? There

was a faint glow of moonlight through the canopy of trees, enough to enable her to make out the small clearing they'd stopped in. There was a stream nearby, and she realized suddenly that she was desperately thirsty, but she couldn't decide whether she dared try to drink some or not.

She couldn't sit here forever. Just long enough to make certain John wasn't coming back. Long enough for the moon to rise a little bit higher and help light her way back to the compound. She had no idea which part of the forest they'd come from, her usual sense of direction had vanished when she needed it most. She fully believed that John could disappear into this jungle and never be seen again, and she hoped he'd be able to do just that.

Unfortunately she fully believed she, too, could get lost and never be seen again, making a tasty meal for whatever creatures roamed the jungle that surrounded them. It wasn't a comforting thought.

She didn't even hear him return. He moved through the night as if he were a part of it, and when he loomed up beside her, his hands full of greenery, she let out a frightened little yelp.

He dropped the stuff in her lap, then sat down cross-legged beside her and began to eat.

The wide green leaves and oddly shaped fruit didn't seem to be bothering him, and she was famished. She took a bite out of the gourdlike fruit, steeling herself for disaster. It wasn't bad. Less sweet than she expected, but starchy and nourishing.

"I'm never leaving fast food again," she muttered underneath her breath as she finished one of the fruits and started in on another. "I'm not cut out for roughing it."

Of course he paid no attention, concentrating on the food. When he'd finished most of it he took a large, flat leaf over to the brook, filling it with water as if it were a cup. To her amazement he brought it back to her, holding it in front of her mouth as tiny droplets splashed on her legs.

"All right," she said. "You win. I'm thirsty." She tried to reach for the leaf, but he refused to let her take it. He simply put it against her mouth, and she had no choice but to drink, deeply, of the fresh, clear water.

There was something strangely disturbing about drinking from his hands, letting him kneel before her. She shook her head when she'd had enough, and the leaf crumbled in his hands, the remaining water splashing down between them.

"Why did you bring me along?" she asked. "Why didn't you leave me back there with the others? I don't belong in the jungle—I'm a city girl, always have been, always will be. All this silence gives me the creeps. I detest camping, I hate the great outdoors, and I want to be back in Chicago

in my own bed. I wish I'd never heard of Edward
J. Hunnicutt and his billions of dollars.''

He just stared at her, and she breathed a sigh of
frustration. ''You don't understand a thing I say, do
you? Why can't I get that through my thick skull?
I was convinced you'd spoken to me last night, that
you asked me to help you. Probably just another
example of the horrors of jet lag.''

He moved a little away from her, sitting back
down again. He was watching her intently, yet with
no understanding in his dark eyes. ''I'm really not
into this you Tarzan, me Jane stuff,'' she said, aim-
ing for cool indifference and falling short. ''It was
nice of you to bring me something to eat, but I'm
not your responsibility. As a matter of fact, I'm
absolutely nothing to you. And I'd like to go back
to the compound now. Don't bother to get up—I
can find the way myself.''

She thought it was worth a try—that she might
at least get a few feet away. He didn't even give
her a chance to stand up, he simply yanked her back
down again. But he released her once she was sitting again, a small comfort. She found the strength
in his rough-skinned, deft hands disturbing.

''All right, maybe you think it's dangerous for
me,'' she said. ''I can accept that. We're obviously
stopping here for the night. In the morning you can
head deeper into the wilderness and I'll find my

way back to the compound. It shouldn't be that difficult, and I'll probably run into a search party.''

He didn't react, and she sighed. "I never realized how frustrating it could be, not being able to talk to people. You're absolutely gorgeous, but you're driving me nuts. Don't you even want to communicate?"

The same, total blankness. "So why did you bring me here?" she demanded. "I still haven't figured that out. I don't think you've suddenly decided you need a mate. I'd hardly be a prime candidate— you need Sheena, Queen of the Jungle, not an over-civilized, overeducated woman like me. And I'm hardly your type. I know my faults, and I have yet to have a man become so enamored with me that he'd carry me off into the wild."

She eyed him warily. "Maybe I shouldn't be quite so outspoken. I'm assuming you don't speak English, but then, there's last night, when I could have sworn you said 'help me.' But it doesn't make sense that you don't try to communicate. You just stare at me as if I'm a brick outhouse. And maybe I'd better continue this conversation in another language."

She switched abruptly. She'd always had a facility for languages, and she was almost as fluent in French as she was in English. "You don't seem the slightest bit interested in the opposite sex," she said in French, and his expression didn't flicker. He knew as much French as he knew English, she thought, depressed. "Not your language, either, eh? I wish to God I knew some obscure Aboriginal languages—some of those might sound familiar. But right now it's like talking to a wall."

John stretched out on the ground like a huge cat, still watching her out of dark, still eyes.

"So you didn't carry me off to mate with me, thank heavens," she continued in French. "You may not even know about sex, if you've been as cut off as everyone suspects. You may not even realize the difference between men and women. You may see me as a slightly prettier version of Mick."

He closed his eyes, and she wondered whether he even heard the sound of her voice as she went on, still in French. "Which is just as well. I certainly wouldn't want you getting ideas. If you know anything about sex at all it would come from watching animals, and I don't feel like replaying *Wild Kingdom* with you. Not that you're asking, of course," she added. He lay very still, peaceful, and the moon went behind a cloud, so that it was too dark for her to see him anymore, even though he was only a few feet away.

"Just as well they're not going to get a chance to drag you off to civilization," she said. "Underneath all that hair you're far too gorgeous for most people to handle. I mean, it's one thing with a scientist like me. I don't react to physical beauty. To me you're nothing more than an experiment. Barely human.

"Yeah, right," she said, disgusted with herself. "If you were barely human I wouldn't have destroyed my career to free you. Years of study, years of hard work down the toilet because I took one look at you and saw a lost little boy, not a missing link. Richard always told me I was too sentimental, and as always, Richard was right."

John had opened his eyes again, watching her without comprehending. "Actually, Richard was an idiot. He thought he should have been the one sent here. You can thank your lucky stars it was a vulnerable fool like me and not Richard. Chances are Richard would have dissected you and harvested your organs before you knew what was happening. He's not troubled with an overburdened sense of humanity or ethics.

"Thank God I didn't marry him. Of course, he was the one who dumped me for that graduate student, but it's just as well. I would have been under his thumb for the rest of my life, and I didn't even like him that much. I just figured I was supposed to marry a scientist and Richard seemed to share my interests. Ha!"

She glanced into the thick tangle of greenery beyond John. "Of course, he wanted the graduate student instead of me because she was built like a model and had a more pliable attitude in just about everything. He didn't even realize she's two years older than me.

"But then, he didn't like that whole child prodigy thing much. He hated the fact that I graduated from college when I was seventeen. He likes to be the high achiever in a relationship. And I let him get away with it, and then he dumped me. More than a year ago, actually, and I haven't done anything but feel relieved and sorry for myself since.

"And here I thought this assignment was going to put my career back on track after Richard derailed it. I was seeing visions of prizes and grants dancing in my head, all with Edward J. Hunnicutt as my patron. It would have worked out beautifully, if only I could have convinced myself that you were a subject, not a human being."

She sighed. "Guess I'm not cut out for that kind of career. Maybe I can find some small rural college that wants an anthropologist and linguistics expert. Or maybe I'll get out of academia all together and find some new field of endeavor. The exciting world of fast food." She shook her head at her own absurdity.

He was still watching her. "You think I'm the crazy one, don't you?" she said in French. "And I guess I am a little nuts right about now. Let's just say it's a lucky thing that either you don't know anything about sex or you simply have the good taste not to be interested in me. Because I have a rotten feeling that if you'd been old and ugly I wouldn't have been quite so eager to risk everything just to see you free. You're too gorgeous for my peace of mind, John, and it would make my life a lot easier if you simply disappeared before I...''

He moved so fast he was like a blur, his body coiling and striking like a huge mountain cat. But he wasn't going after an enemy. He simply crossed the space between them, caught her face in his hand and tilted it up to his.

There was no recognition in his dark, merciless eyes. No understanding or acknowledgement in his face. There was only his mouth, pressed against hers before she had even the faintest idea what he intended.

She was too shocked to do anything but hold very still, while he kissed her mouth, silencing her spate of words that he couldn't understand. He tasted like clean water and the fruit they'd shared, and his mouth was cool and wet against hers, and for a moment she let herself drift with the strange wonder of it, ready to open her mouth for him, ready for anything, when reality intruded with shocking suddenness, and she reached up, put her hands against the warm, bare chest that she realized she'd been wanting to touch for a lifetime, and she shoved him away from her.

He fell back gracefully, as if he'd expected her

to stop him, and his face was empty and still, as distant and removed as it had ever been.

"Why did you do that?" she demanded in a hushed voice. "How did you even know how to do that? Who the hell are you?"

He hadn't moved away, and she was suddenly terrified that he wasn't going to. That he was going to kiss her again, and she was going to let him. Going to open her mouth for him, going to let him put his strong, deft hands all over her body, touch her as she wanted him to touch her, and the thought horrified her. She wanted him. She hadn't even realized that simple, basic lust had been lurking beneath her concern like an ugly parasite.

And all he had to do was touch her again, kiss her again, and she'd probably rip off her own clothes, to lie with him in the jungle, to drink in the taste and the scent of him, to hide against the smooth, hot flesh of his strong body.

She had to keep that from happening. His deep, fathomless eyes stared into hers, and in moments he'd touch her again, and she'd be lost. She had no defenses, nothing to keep him away, not even the meager defense of words, when suddenly she remembered the tranquilizer darts. She'd shoved a handful in one of the cargo pockets of her pants right before she left—she could grab one, flick off the cap and stab him with it if he came near her again. It would be simple enough, and the only way to save herself.

Not from him. But from her own, shockingly base, wild instincts.

He uncurled from his sitting position, and she was certain he was going to touch her again. She shoved her hand in her pocket, searching for the darts, when something sharp pricked against her finger.

She jerked her hand out, to see one of the darts had come uncapped and buried itself in her hand.

"Oh, sh—" But before she could finish the word she passed out cold, at the wild man's narrow, bare feet.

Chapter Eight

John Bartholomew Hunter looked down at the woman at his feet. He didn't need to see the barb sticking in her hand to know that she'd been knocked out by the tranquilizer darts. He'd felt the sting in his hide far too often, experienced the sickening loss of consciousness not to recognize the symptoms. She was out cold.

He squatted down beside her, pushing her short cropped hair out of her face to get a better look at her. He generally liked women with long hair, with robust, curvy bodies, women tall like he was. He'd heard them say her name. Doctor Elizabeth Holden was much too short for him, too skinny, and her thick golden hair barely reached her ears.

She had a gorgeous mouth, though. That was one of the first things he'd noticed about her, as he lay strapped to that goddamned gurney where they tied him every day. He'd been able to steal glances at her while he should have been completely out of it, and it was her mouth that had drawn him. Wide, generous, with a touch of vulnerability about it that started the most amazing erotic fantasies. After all, what else did he have to do while he was strapped there but fantasize? Fortunately he'd had enough self-control, despite the damned drugs, to wait until she'd left—she'd been poking and checking his body so carefully that his physical reaction to the thought of her mouth would have given her quite a start.

He still didn't trust her. Anyone working for the bastard who'd brought him to this place had to prove their trustworthiness. So she let him out of that prison. That didn't mean she wouldn't go screeching for help when the going got tough.

He should have left her behind, but he knew exactly what would have happened. Alf was a nasty piece of goods, and he derived a lot of pleasure out of inflicting pain. Mick was harmless, but he couldn't stand up to Alf. It wouldn't take much to get the truth out of a little thing like Libby. And he couldn't in good conscience leave her behind to face their wrath. He owed her that much.

She wasn't particularly grateful. She'd been fighting him since he'd hauled her out of the hell-hole, and she'd probably run off the first chance she got. Which was why he had no intention of giving her a chance. She didn't have an ounce of common sense as far as he could see, and she was just as likely to stumble off a cliff or eat some poisoned fruit as she was to get back safely.

He sat down beside her, pulled her limp body up against his and put her head in his lap. He felt oddly tender. Probably a normal enough reaction after what had to be months of sophisticated torture, when he had no voice to stop them, no way to tell them they were making a mistake. After a while, when he thought he might be able to communicate, he'd thought better of it. What would they do when it came out that they'd kidnapped and imprisoned him, all on the supposition that he was a wild forest creature, more animal than human? Somehow they thought they had the right. And he wouldn't have put it past Alf to cover up untidy mistakes like kidnapping him in the simplest way possible. Bodies decomposed very quickly in this climate, and from what he'd been able to overhear, Hunnicutt had bought the entire island and shipped the few inhabitants off it.

They hadn't discovered his way off it, though, or they would have known who he was. So with any luck there was a still a way out of this place before Hunnicutt and his hired thugs found him. Them.

He looked down at Libby, absently stroking her hair. And he tried his ruined voice. "You're quite a brave one, aren't you, love?" he said, his voice no more than a cracked whisper. It had been coming back for a while now, and he'd been practicing at night, when they let the dope wear off before they caught him again, hunted him like the wild animal they believed, or at least hoped, him to be.

He wasn't up to his full strength—they'd been bleeding him for too long. God only knows what use they thought his blood would be. It was chock full of the dope they used on him, the injections and the tranquilizer darts—hardly the liquid gold Alf was crowing about. Maybe Hunnicutt was a closet vampire and he wanted pure blood to keep him going. Except if he drank his blood he'd end up being as zonked as his captive was.

No, there were no vampires around here. No missing links either. There was a perfectly reasonable explanation for his presence here, if over the years that he had come and gone anyone had bothered to ask. Though there was always the chance he wouldn't have bothered to answer. He didn't have a whole lot of patience with stupid questions, or people. He needed a certain amount of solitude to survive, and anyone who interfered with it was likely to discover that John Bartholomew Hunter could be very rude indeed.

She was deeply drugged, her head in his lap, her eyes closed. She had pretty eyes too, and he'd plenty of chances to stare blankly into them while he had been lying there drugged.

By tomorrow most of the drugs should be out of

his system. By tomorrow it would have been long enough since they last took blood that he'd probably be close to full strength. Just being free had energized him, but his strength was beginning to fade. She was small, but even lugging an extra hundred pounds through the jungle after a long stretch of limited activity had unexpectedly worn him out.

He tilted his head back, looking at the night sky through the canopy of trees, breathing in the fresh, humid air as a ripple of pure pleasure ran through his body. He'd always known he needed freedom and the thick tropical wilderness at regular intervals to keep him balanced. He'd never realized just how necessary it was for his very sanity. A few more weeks in that prison and he might not have been able to come back from that dark place in his mind.

He leaned down, breathing in the scent of her skin. When he first stepped outside that prison he thought he could run forever. Now his energy had disappeared, and there was nothing he could do but lie down and wait until it returned.

He stretched out on the soft, spongy ground, taking her with him, wrapping his body around her to protect her against the night. She wasn't made for this, more's the pity. She belonged in her cities, not in his jungle. He'd have to see she got back there.

In the meantime, though, he'd lie with his arms around her, breathing in the scent of her skin, tickled by her short, curly hair, aroused by the deceptively fragile bone and muscle of her. She'd done better than he would have expected in keeping up with him. She was stronger than she looked.

She was also stubborn, distrustful, and she had absolutely no idea what she was dealing with when she looked at him and started reeling off things she wouldn't have told her therapist. In English, the language of his birth, in French, his mother's language and his own second tongue. He'd listened to her litany with his stalwart expression, trying to resist the impulse to kiss her.

In the end he'd given in to that impulse, which was probably a major mistake. Missing links didn't kiss, did they? She'd probably start wondering where he'd come up with notion, and then she'd remember he'd spoken to her, and then there'd be questions that he wasn't about to answer. He didn't trust her. It was that simple.

She made a soft, moaning sound in her deep, drugged sleep, and he wrapped his arms around her, cradling her. ''Go to sleep, love,'' he whispered in his raw voice. ''It'll be morning soon enough, and you can hate me all over again. You'll like that, won't you? Gives you reason to feel something.'' His voice was getting stronger all the time. He didn't know if it would ever be the same as it was before some bastard had wrapped a rope around his throat and nearly choked him to death, but at least he was getting better.

She snuggled against him, seeking warmth in the tropical night, and he pulled her closer. In her own way she was as shut off as he was, and now they were thrown together, running... Were they running for their lives? It was entirely possible, and he wasn't about to take any chances. The sooner he got off this island, and took the woman with him, the better.

He was so damned tired. He'd lost track of time long ago, but he was guessing they'd held him captive for more than a month. He would have thought that a month of drugged sleep would have been enough to last him, but right now he knew he couldn't move a step further, particularly not carrying a hundred plus pounds of dead weight. And even if he could, he didn't want to.

He wanted to lie with a woman in his arms, breathing in the cooling air of the jungle night. He wanted to close his eyes and know that when he woke up he'd still be free. For now, that was enough.

Libby was having the oddest dreams. She knew they were dreams, even as she was having them, so she didn't let them disturb her too deeply. After all, how ridiculous could it be, to think she'd be lost in a jungle, sleeping with some kind of nearly-naked, god-like savage? She didn't bother fighting the strange visions that flitted through her heavily sleeping mind—it would have done no good, and maybe there was something to be learned from the fantasies. Her sweet, mildly flaky mother had always insisted that dreams were a message from the spirits.

If this was a message she couldn't even begin to understand what it was trying to tell her, but she dutifully let the dreams come, trying to remember them for the morning when she'd wake up in her own safe bed and try to figure out what they meant.

She knew what the nearly naked man meant—that part was simple. Lust. It was a subject she was relatively unfamiliar with, and obviously her subconscious decided she needed a little erotic stimulation. The living, breathing body wrapped around hers was an undeniably potent fantasy, and since he wasn't real she might as well enjoy it, enjoy the unfamiliar feeling of someone protecting her, taking care of her. A fantasy creature who was as arousing as he was imaginary.

The dreams grew stranger as the night wore on, which was only to be expected. She opened her eyes to see a huge pig standing a few feet away, looking at her out of mad, dark piggy eyes. At least she assumed it was a pig. She heard a voice, rumbling against her chest so that it seemed to come from inside her, telling the pig that they were no danger to him, and that he could go away and leave them alone.

And after a moment the pig left, and Libby

closed her eyes again to ponder this new absurdity. Had she been talking to the pig, or had it been the voice of God? What had the pig symbolized in her life—she couldn't begin to imagine.

And stranger still, the rough voice spoke French with an Australian accent.

She gave up then, drifting back to sleep, snuggling closer to her imaginary protector, reveling in the heat of his smooth, strong body. Nothing was going to harm her, not French speaking pigs, not Richard with his casual rejection, not Edward J. Hunnicutt and his haphazard grants and jobs and revenge.

The thought of Hunnicutt almost woke her up, but sleep won out. She should remember something, beware of something, but it eluded her, and in the end she slept, safe and sound, in a pleasant state of perfectly innocent desire for the imaginary man beside her.

It was broad daylight when she opened her eyes, and she blinked, trying to focus on the green mist in front of her. It took her long moments to realize she wasn't in a bed, and longer moments to realize she wasn't alone. Someone was holding her, a strong body was behind her, and when she tried to sit up in sudden panic his hold tightened on her, keeping her still.

It came back to her with such a rushing force that she almost passed out again. She'd drugged

Mick and Alf, and set the wild man free. Except that he'd decided to take her with him, carting her off into the middle of nowhere, and now here she was, curled up with him like a kitten.

She couldn't quite remember how she'd gotten to this particular place. She remembered he'd carried her for what seemed like hours, and then they stopped for the night. She had another memory, but it couldn't have been real. It must have had something to do with the French pig. Surely a wild creature like John couldn't have kissed her. Couldn't have even known what kissing was.

She'd dreamed it, she decided flatly. Along with the pig and the strange voice. Maybe it had been the pig speaking, though its mouth hadn't moved. Maybe it was the voice of her guardian angel, though why her angel would have the raspy voice of a barfly and speak French with an Australian accent was beyond her comprehension.

"I need to get up," she said in a low, firm voice. He didn't move. Of course he didn't—he didn't understand a word she said. She tugged against his encompassing hold, trying to demonstrate. "I need to get up," she said again.

After a moment he released her, and she scrambled away from him. Her body didn't seem to want to obey her commands—it felt stiff, sluggish, and belatedly she remembered the spiny dart in her hand. If she remembered that, maybe her memory of the kiss had been real as well.

She looked at him, but he looked the same. Remote, expressionless. If he had any understanding beneath that face she had yet to reach it.

She started to stand up, and he reached for her, to pull her back down. He caught her wrist, the bruised one, and she let out an involuntary yelp of pain. Enough to startle him into releasing her.

"I have to go to the bathroom," she said. "In the woods. Alone."

He didn't blink. For the first time she could see his eyes in bright light, without the drugs and artificial darkness. They were brown, a rich, chocolate brown, and even without expression they were as decadently seductive as a box of Godiva chocolates. Libby had spent her life resisting any sort of temptation. Her one failure was Godiva chocolates.

She took a step back, and he didn't grab her. "I have to go…" Words failed her. She wasn't about to act it out for him, and she certainly wasn't going to squat in the woods with him watching.

"Stay there!" she said firmly, holding up her hand in a halting gesture, once more thinking of Lassie. Though sitting there in the sunlight, John looked a far cry from a faithful canine companion. A wolf, maybe, but nothing tame.

Thank God he didn't move. She wasn't sure what she would have done if he tried to stop her, or follow her. She dove through the underbrush, careful not to go too far, finding a small, private spot and relief.

Only for a minute did she consider trying to take off, escape from her captor. The problem was, she had no idea which direction to go. If she ran, he'd probably catch her, and if he did, he'd never give her a scant moment's privacy again.

She thrashed her way back to the clearing, making as much noise as she could, only to find the place deserted when she got there. So much for her worries, she thought, kneeling down at the stream and cupping her hands for a drink. It was cool and clear and delicious. Almost as delicious as when he'd held it for her last night.

"Stop it," she said out loud. "Too many erotic fantasies." The words were no sooner out of her mouth than John reappeared in the clearing, once more bearing those strange, breadlike fruits. "And thank God you don't understand a word I say," she added, sitting back on her heels. "You don't need to know I'm having ridiculously lustful feelings. Obviously I've lost my mind. Maybe it's the Stockholm syndrome, where the victim falls in love with her kidnapper. No, I don't think that's it. To be perfectly honest, I've been having unprofessional fantasies since I first saw you, and I don't know if I can keep blaming the time difference. All I can do is thank God you don't understand a word I say.''

He handed her one of the fruits that they'd shared last night, and she bit into it, savoring the salty-sweet taste of it. "You know, this is very good," she said, as he sat down across from her and began to eat. "A far cry from an Egg McMuffin, but very nice."

He was ignoring her as he concentrated on his breakfast, and she stretched out her legs in front of her. "God, I feel grimy," she said with a sigh. "I'm wearing twice the clothes you are, and I'm not cut out for running through the jungle. I do realize you carted me for hours, but I'm still feeling achy and grungy. I would kill for a hot bath, a good bed and a Big Mac."

He kept eating. "You aren't really that different from Richard, you know," she continued in a conversational tone. "He never paid any attention to anything I said, either. Except, of course, for my theory on the tribesmen of Whachua. Did I tell you Richard and I were in the same field? Unfortunately Richard never had an original thought in his entire life, so he simply borrowed mine. And I, stupid idiot that I am, was honored that I could contribute to his work. All without credit, of course."

John had finished his breakfast and was looking at her from those still, watchful eyes. But for some reason Libby couldn't stop talking. The silence was driving her nuts.

"I should have realized when the sex was bad," she continued chattily. "I suppose it might have improved with practice, but after the third or fourth time I just gave up. I've never been particularly lucky when it comes to sex. I don't think I'm a very sensual person." She licked the last taste of the fruit off her lips with a small, satisfied sigh. He was staring at her, and she smiled.

"And you don't understand a word I'm saying," she said with surprising cheer. "And a good thing, too. This is like therapy—I can tell you my darkest secrets, get them off my chest and no one will know but me."

He rose, indifferent to her chatter, waiting for her to rise, too. She figured she had no choice, and she wasn't sure she wanted him to touch her. His touch was unnerving. "Are we going?" she asked brightly. "I suppose so. Well, you lead the way and I'll tell you all about my childhood while we walk. After all, I might as well get some use out of this trek apart from the physical exercise. Then we'll get to my neurotic adolescence, ending up with my lousy sex life. And then I'll start fantasizing about how you spent your life."

He'd started to walk away, but at that point he turned back to her, and for a brief moment she thought she saw the glimmer of an expression in his eyes. So brief that it vanished before she could even begin to decipher it.

"I'm coming," she said, following after him. "But you might answer me one question."

He'd turned and started walking, and she ran to keep up with him through the dense greenery. It was too thick to walk abreast, so she stayed behind him while he pushed the fronds out of the way.

"You don't have to answer me, of course. And you won't. But I just wondered if it was my imagination, or did you really kiss me last night?"

As she expected, there was no answer. He just moved deeper into the jungle. And she followed after him, lapsing into silence, remembering.

Chapter Nine

If there was one thing John Bartholomew Hunter couldn't abide, it was a chatty woman. And yet here he was, tromping through the rain forest with someone who couldn't stop talking, who seemed determined to share every intimate detail of her life with her supposedly uncomprehending companion, and on top of that, he was fascinated. From her activist parents who'd adored her, through her high school and college years when she was always at least five years younger than her classmates. No dates, no proms, though she didn't seem particularly saddened by their lack. She seemed more disturbed by the lack of sex in her life. Whoever Richard was, he certainly hadn't done right by her.

And of course she blamed herself. She was too intellectual to be passionate, she said reasonably as she scrambled behind him through the foliage. It was amazing that she'd developed such a healthy case of lust for him, and she was enjoying herself immensely, just watching him, secure in the knowledge that he had no idea she was having erotic fantasies about him, probably had no idea what erotic fantasies were in the first place. If he'd lived a life in the jungle, without other people around, he probably didn't even know what sex was.

And John wondered how long he'd hold back before he jumped on her and showed her exactly how mistaken she was. At least it would silence her for a bit.

The drugs must have had a longer-lasting effect than he would have thought. There was no reason for him to be contemplating having sex with Dr. Elizabeth Holden, and he was doing a lot more than contemplating. He was using all his concentration to keep from touching her, because he knew once he did it would be all over.

They should reach the coast by late afternoon if they were lucky. If not, it would still be by midnight, and he had excellent night vision. They could leave, and then he could get rid of her, somehow or other, all without saying a word. He was good at disappearing, and she'd be able to find her way back to the States, to the cities and the fast food that she needed.

If he could keep his hands off her.

Eventually she stopped talking, and while the silence was more restful, it left him free to think too much. About her. About how he'd gotten to this place. And about how he was going to deal with Edward J. Hunnicutt and his thugs.

Something had to be done. He was free, and no one would touch him again. But a man like Hunnicutt thought rules didn't apply to him and living beings were simply put on earth for his curiosity. He needed to be taught a hard lesson in life. And his minions as well.

Besides, if he didn't, they might very well go after Libby. For all she seemed ready to give up her career, he knew perfectly well that was not a viable option. He didn't want Hunnicutt wielding his dollars to destroy her life. He needed to protect her as much as he needed to protect the other helpless things that might cross Hunnicutt's path.

Not that Libby was particularly helpless. She could probably talk him to death. John felt a small, reluctant smile tug at his mouth at the thought. She had a nice voice, slightly husky, though nothing compared to the ravaged croak he managed to make. God help him, he'd begun to miss her chattering.

It was logical enough. None of his captors had spoken a word to him. He could hear them talking among themselves through his drugged daze, more than they could ever have imagined. But until she put her hands on his body, spoke to him in her soft, husky voice, he hadn't had anyone treat him like a human being.

He heard the sounds of the waterfall in the distance, and he breathed a sigh of relief. Not that he'd doubted his instincts—normally he could have found his way across the island in pitch-black and pouring rain. But right now he wasn't trusting anything to be as it should, and it was a consolation that at least he knew where he was going.

The waterfall and pool were only a few hours inland from the beach—if their luck held they'd be out of there by nightfall. He glanced back at his companion. She was starting to limp slightly, and she looked exhausted. That unexpected dose of the tranquilizer dart hadn't helped her energy level, though it had at least ensured a good night's sleep. If she'd started chattering about her unsatisfactory love life last night he might have done something about it. Something they'd both regret.

Her senses weren't nearly as attuned as his were, but even she began to realize they were approaching water. She moved faster to catch up with him, and he half expected her to take his hand. She stopped herself in time, and he knew why. She wanted to avoid touching him for almost the same reason he wanted to avoid touching her. She was afraid of where it might lead. He knew exactly where.

"Is that water?" she asked. "It smells like water. Are we near the ocean?"

He didn't answer, he just kept plowing onward through the thick growth, surreptitiously holding the greenery so it wouldn't thwack her in the face. In her state of exhaustion even a palm frond might knock her over. She needed a chance to rest, she needed cool water to swim in and drink, she needed something to eat. And she needed him to keep his distance so he wouldn't see that confused, longing expression in her blue eyes.

That was another thing. He didn't like blue-eyed women, either. He liked his woman tall, curvy, exotic and mysterious. Not a little puppy dog who blurted out the intimate details of her life and speculated on his with disarming candor.

Of course, she had no idea she was being candid with anyone but herself. And he wasn't sure whether he was going to tell her or not. By now he had almost decided she wouldn't betray him, but he'd been through too much in the last unknown period of time to trust lightly. Besides, the less she knew the better. It would probably be best for her if he simply faded into the rain forest. That way she could still have her erotic fantasies unsullied by the usually less-than-satisfactory reality.

Though he couldn't help thinking that at least he could provide her with a better reality than Richard, whoever the hell he was.

Dangerous thoughts, he reminded himself, keeping his expression stoic, and he pushed through the last bit of clearing to the pool. He heard her hushed intake of breath, and suddenly he was transported back, almost twenty-five years ago, when he had first found this place. His reaction had been the same, wonder and delight, at a time when staying alive had been his full-time occupation.

"Oh, my God, it's beautiful," Libby said. He glanced down at her, but her attention was on the wide expanse of lagoon, the waterfall sending ripples across the smooth surface.

"I don't care what you say, I'm going swimming," she said, pushing past him. She paused at the edge, turning back to look at him. "Of course you're not going to say anything, are you? But I imagine you'd know whether this lagoon is filled with piranhas or water moccasins or the like, and you'd stop me from going in if it was dangerous. Wouldn't you?"

He didn't answer. Instead he dove into the water, straight past her, deliberately splashing her.

From under the water he heard her shriek, and then her splash as she followed him. She was either a lousy diver or she'd done a cannonball, he thought, kicking his legs and skimming beneath the surface. One small woman shouldn't have been able to make that big a splash. He'd better keep an eye on her in case she was a lousy swimmer. He surfaced, but there was no sign of her, and he knew a moment's panic. He dove back under immediately, only to come face-to-face with her under the water as she moved silently through the clear blue.

He froze, as did she, in that silent underwater universe. And then she kicked to the surface, and he moved away, to make certain that when he came up for air he wouldn't be anywhere near her.

He'd underestimated her effect on him. A few inches closer in that warm, sweet water and he would have…might have…

It was absurd. After all these years he knew himself and his body very well, and his self-control and self-will were phenomenal. If need be he could go without food, without water, without rest, without sleep. The thought of giving in to temptation with a woman who was disaster for him was unthinkable.

And he couldn't stop thinking about it.

The water was doing little to cool him off. She was over by the waterfall, and he could see that she was a strong, good swimmer. She didn't need him hovering, making sure she didn't drown. On land he needed to stay near. In the water they were on equal terms. He had no reason to go anywhere near the waterfall.

She'd found the bit of ledge and climbed out on it, so that she stood beneath the stream of water, head tilted back, letting it pour over her body. He'd tried very hard not to pay attention to her body, but right now that was proving impossible. She'd been wearing a baggy pair of khakis and a white T-shirt when he'd dragged her out of the house. And a bra—he could see that quite clearly through the soaking, stretched-out T-shirt. A lace bra that hooked in the front. And she was curvier than he'd realized.

The khakis had sagged down low on her hips, and she grabbed the tail of her T-shirt to wring it out, exposing her stomach. John made a little moaning sound in the water that was thankfully covered by the sound of the falls. Determinedly he tried to think of other women, but nothing could distract him. He simply treaded water, staring at her.

She hadn't realized he was watching her. She ran her hands through her short hair, rubbing the water into it, then pulled open the neck of her T-shirt to let the water stream underneath it. She was gloriously, unself-consciously female, reveling in the water and the sun and the day, and all he could do was watch her.

In the end, it might have saved their lives. If he'd been where he wanted to be, with her under the pounding water, he never would have heard their approach. The two men who'd held him prisoner for so long were arguing, idiotically unaware they were signaling their arrival. Even if they thought he was nothing more than a wild beast they should have realized his natural defenses were well-honed.

He immediately dove under the water, swimming rapidly across the width of the lagoon to the waterfall. Without warning he surged up next to Libby, shocking a little squeak out of her before he covered her mouth with his hand, dragging her under the waterfall into the water-splashed darkness of the shallow cave.

She was struggling again, and he couldn't blame her, but he couldn't let her give away their presence. He had no choice but to restrain her, pushing her down on the rock ledge, imprisoning her body with his much larger one so she could barely struggle. She bit his hand, hard, but he didn't react, lying motionless on top of her as he listened for the voices that were dangerously close.

And then she heard the voices as well, and she stopped struggling, stopped trying to bite him, almost stopped breathing.

"What makes you think they came this way?" the little man's voice floated down to them. "We've been circling this area for hours now. If you ask me they're closer to the house. He was too drugged to make it very far."

"But I didn't ask you, now did I?" The bigger, meaner one said. "You still think he kidnapped the little darling, when I know she's had the hots for him the moment she laid eyes on him. Never trust a woman, I always say, and the quiet, smart ones are the worst. They always go the wildest when they break out.''

"But she's not like that," Mick said plaintively. "She's just got a soft heart when it comes to creatures like him…''

"Not likely," the big one, Alf, snorted. "She's with him, all right, and it was her idea. And she's not going to be happy when we finally catch up with the two of them. Which we will, or my name isn't Alf Droggan.''

"Er… actually your name is Orville Johnson, Alf. We've been mates since we were in school together, and you changed it after you'd been nicked for…''

"Shut up, Mick. That doesn't alter the fact that we'll find them, and soon.''

"You still haven't told me what you're planning to do with them. Assuming we find them together, and that he hasn't hurt her. You don't think he would have hurt her, do you, Alf? After all, he broke your arm in three places.''

"I know he broke my arm in three places, Mick.'' Alf's patience was clearly wearing thin. They must have stopped just above the waterfall, and he was having to shout to be heard. Loud enough that John and Libby could understand every word as they lay entwined in the darkness. "And no, I don't think he's hurt her. Not the way I'm going to hurt her when I catch up with them.''

"You can't, Alf!" Mick protested.

"Watch me. Dr. Elizabeth Holden has just proven herself a major liability and a royal pain in the arse, and I don't think she's the type to take a payoff and be quiet, do you? She's one of those idealistic do-gooder types who'll go running off to the newspapers or some wildlife organization screaming bloody murder. And I can think of only one way to stop her.''

"Bloody murder?" Mick said in a mournful voice.

"And who told you you weren't very bright?" Alf said cheerfully.

"You do, Alf. All the time."

"Never mind that, Mick. We've got to find the two of them. We've got to get rid of the lady, get Tarzan back in the lab before Hunnicutt finds out something's happened.''

"But won't he wonder what happened to her?"

"He knows enough not to ask questions. I just wish I could say the same for you, Mick, me lad. He didn't question it when Dr. McDonough took his little tumble, now did he? He told me Mc-Donough was a liability and he needed to be gotten rid of. I took care of it, no questions asked. That's why he hired the lady—he knew she had no one to come asking questions about her. By the time anyone realizes she's disappeared everything will be so covered up it would take an archaeologist to find out anything."

"But why would an archaeologist go looking?" Mick said plaintively. "Ow, that hurt!"

"Then stop asking stupid questions. And stop worrying about the bitch doctor. She betrayed us, and she'll get what's coming to her."

"I still wish we didn't have to hurt her," Mick said.

"You're too bleeding softhearted, you are. And it's getting late. I want to find them before sundown if I can."

"They can't get off the island, can they?"

"Not unless they want to be shark-bait. We're a hundred miles from any other land. They're sitting ducks. We'll find 'em, sooner or later."

"Just do me a favor, would you, Alf?" Mick's voice was plaintive.

"What now?"

"Don't hurt her. Kill her quickly, just a good clean snap of the neck. I don't want her to suffer."

"I can always let you do the honors, pally."

"No, thanks anyway," Mick said hastily. "You do it. I'll just watch. Which way are we headed?"

"We'll go east from here. Sooner or later we'll come across some sign of them."

"Right," said Mick cheerfully, his voice fading away. "But are you sure we have to …?"

John waited long, endless minutes, unmoving. He knew enough not to trust them—life was full of coincidences and conveniences but he never took them for granted. From the sound of it Mick and Alf had been carrying on that argument from the moment they left the house, and they would have overheard a good part of it any time they came close. But he still wasn't taking any chances.

Libby lay small and still beneath him in the darkness. She was trembling, random shivers running through her body, and he wished he could dare warm her, dare reassure her, even take his hand from her mouth. But he couldn't. He was living on adrenaline alone, and he wasn't about to risk exposing her to Alf's bloodthirsty anger. He was bigger and stronger than Alf, but the man almost certainly had a gun. And probably loaded with something a bit more lethal than tranquilizer darts.

At least the stupid fools hadn't managed to track them. John had been doing the best he could not to leave any trace. He could see his own trail plain as day, but Alf and Mick weren't as experienced. They were headed away from them, thank God. They just had to stay in the cave a little while longer, to make certain they were safe.

She was shaking harder now, trembling in his arms. Her clothes were sopping wet, chilling her despite the jungle heat, and even his body warmth wasn't helping. He raised his head, looking down into her panicked eyes. He moved his hand away from her mouth, ready to clamp it back if she made the slightest sound.

Her lips, her erotic, delicious lips were trembling with cold and fear, and she looked up at him as if she thought he could save her, as if he were the answer to every question in the universe. She looked up at him in silent, blind panic. And then she put her hands on his head and pulled his mouth down to hers.

Chapter Ten

In the end, he didn't know how it happened, and he didn't particularly care. She was shaking so hard, with cold and with fear, that all he could think of was he had to warm her. She was clutching him with her small hands, kissing him with that luscious, sweet mouth of hers, and there was never any question of what he was going to do.

He pulled the soaking, stretched-out T-shirt over her head and tossed it to one side, unhooked the front clasp of her bra with a deft gesture. In the darkness he could barely see her, but it didn't matter. He could touch her, feel her, the small, tender breasts, nipples hard from cold rather than desire. He knew a moment's hesitation, his brain kicking in for one last protest, and then she reached down and shoved her khakis and underwear off, and she was naked beneath him in the shadowed cave, and it was far too late.

"Please," she said in a panicked voice as she kissed him, awkward, hurried kisses.

She was going to shake apart with cold and fear, and he was going to explode from smothered desire, and he abandoned the last remnants of his conscience, kicked out of his shorts and covered her.

He wanted to kiss her, but she wouldn't let him. She wasn't aroused, she was terrified, and he didn't want to take her that way, but there was no choice, between her panic and his simple lust. He slid between her legs and she clutched at him, pulling him into her, and he gave up fighting, gave over to the sheer, physical sensation of her body, sinking deep into its welcoming tightness.

He almost climaxed immediately, but he had enough self-control left to stop himself, to slow it down. Her shaking had stopped—now she seemed frozen beneath him, and he started to pull out, guilty.

"No!" she cried, clawing at him, pulling him back. "Finish it!" Her eyes were closed, and tears were streaming down her face, but she clamped her legs around him, trying to hurry him.

He tried to touch her face, but she shook his hand away. He didn't know what she needed, what she wanted, and in the end it didn't matter. They couldn't turn back now, and in truth, neither of them wanted to.

He caught her hips in his hands, pulling her up

against him, and he began to move, deep, measured strokes, steady, as he tried to lure her from that nightmare of panic she'd retreated to. He took his time, letting it build, deeper, harder, until he felt her dampen around him, felt her breathing change and her heart quicken, felt the hot stirrings of real desire begin to wash through her.

And he fed it, teasing her, coaxing her with nothing more than the act of sex. She wouldn't let him touch her anywhere else, but he didn't need to. She was beginning to gasp, and her body was tightening around his, and he knew, unbelievably, that she was on the very edge of climaxing. He could feel the shivers of reaction dancing across her skin, feel the beginning quivers of her orgasm, and he pushed in deep, needing her, wanting to fill her completely, wanting to join her.

And then she stopped. Froze, the moment the first shiver of climax hit her, but it was too late for him. He went rigid, exploding inside her, groaning deep in his throat from pleasure and regret.

He sank down on her, the rock ledge sharp beneath his knees and elbows, as he tried to control his breathing. He didn't know what to say to her, and then, after a moment, he remembered that he didn't have to say anything at all. As far as she knew, he couldn't speak, couldn't understand a thing she said.

He was half-prepared when she shoved him off

her—he'd been trying to keep his full weight from crushing her against the rock ledge—and he rolled away easily as she scrambled out from underneath him. He saw her naked body for a brief moment as it flashed by, and then she disappeared through the waterfall, into the cool depths of the lagoon, presumably to wash every trace of him off of her, out of her.

He sat up, slowly, and began cursing. Out loud— silent curses weren't nearly as satisfying. He'd spent most of his civilized life in Australia, and the Australians were expert at cursing. The raw, muttered syllables would have shocked a sailor, but he took scant pleasure in it.

How could he have been so stupid? There'd been other ways to calm her, other ways to warm her, but no, he had to go right for the gold, no matter how yappy and neurotic she was. No matter how vulnerable. He'd had sex with her before he'd ever held a conversation with her. He'd had hot, fast, dirty sex with her when she was the type who'd want a bed strewn with roses. He needed someone to give him a good swift kick in the ass.

On top of that, he hadn't used any protection. Funny thing, that. He didn't happen to carry condoms when he'd been held captive and was running for his life, and neither did she.

He washed off under the waterfall, discreetly out of sight, then pulled his shorts back on. Her wet clothes lay scattered on the narrow ledge, and he scooped them up, planning to carry them out into the sunlight to help them dry a bit. The skimpy little bra was on top, and when he realized he was absently stroking it, he dropped it on the ground, only to have the stream of the waterfall catch it and drag it away. He made no effort to retrieve it.

She was at the far end of the lagoon, swimming, and he knew she wouldn't turn to face him. She'd probably stay in the water until her body temperature dropped to a dangerous level, and he'd have to haul her out by force. Maybe even perform mouth-to-mouth resuscitation on her, and there was no question where that would lead.

The best he could do for her right now was ignore her. He spread her clothes across some of the bushes where the hot sun could get them, feeling something hard in one of the pockets. At first he thought it might have been an overlooked tranquilizer dart, but when he zipped open the tiny pocket he found a small but perfectly serviceable Swiss Army knife. Nice of her to mention it, he thought wryly, tucking it into his own pocket. Had she forgotten she had it, or did she think she might have to end up stabbing him? After this afternoon's debacle she might be sorely tempted to do just that.

She was swimming laps, a fool thing to do when she was already half-exhausted from their hike through the rain forest. He stood in the shadows, watching her pale body glide through the transparent water, and he tried to tell himself what he felt was regret. When he knew damned well what he was feeling was desire. He wanted her again, he wanted her on a bed, all night long, where he could take his time and make her come until she was ready to pass out from it. He wanted an absolute orgy with her pale, naked body—that brief, barely satisfactory coupling behind the waterfall had only turned his sexual appetite into a voracious monster. He'd been planning on getting rid of her as soon as they got off this place—he knew that was what she wanted, especially after today. She needed cities and civilization like a drunkard needed whiskey.

And he knew he wasn't going to be able to let her go. Not right away. Not with things unfinished between them.

He stretched out a ways from the lagoon, a spot where she could see him, know that he wasn't watching her. He needed to lull her into at least a truce. She probably hated him for this afternoon. He didn't blame her.

But he had every intention of changing her mind.

AT LEAST SHE'D STOPPED crying, Libby thought, pushing her body through the cool water with merciless determination. Nothing could stop her feelings of abject shame, the water couldn't even begin to cool the blush of embarrassment that swamped her body. What in God's name had come over her? She'd never done anything like that in her entire life. With a stranger. Someone who was closer to a wild animal than a man. In fact, she'd forced him, though he'd raised no objections. The memory of his hard, muscled flesh straining over her, the feel of him inside her, was still tormenting her, and all the water in the world wouldn't wash away that feeling.

She hadn't let him kiss her. She'd been afraid to, though she wasn't sure why. She'd needed sex— for the first time in her entire life she'd needed a man, and she'd taken the one who was available.

Of course, she was ignoring the fact that she'd been having fantasies about him since she first saw him. He wasn't a casual stranger she happened to jump. She'd been acutely, intensely aware of him and his body for days now. It wasn't general panic that had made her jump him, and there was no other word for it. It was specific, directed at him. He'd brought her out of that place, he'd protected her. And some deep, primitive part of her wanted that protection guaranteed. She wanted to be claimed, so that he wouldn't let her go easily.

All the silly little games women played, and she could see them in the harsh light of day, and feel like a fool. The sooner she got off this island, away from him, the better. Her fear of Alf and Mick was nothing compared to her fear of John. Her fear of what she was feeling.

She needed the city, the sidewalks, the cold chill of winter sinking into her bones. She wasn't made for wild adventures with wild creatures. She was made for safety and comfort and security. Wasn't she?

The flash of white caught her eye, and she spun in the water, suddenly nervous, to see her clothes stretched out on the bushes, drying. He was nowhere to be seen—a small blessing. She'd have to face him sooner or later, but she was in no hurry. She'd be able to regain her equilibrium eventually. That feverish coupling beneath the waterfall had been a one-time aberration. She'd get over it. As for John, he'd clearly known what he was doing, which ruled out the possibility that he'd lived his entire life isolated from other people. At some point or another he'd been around women, and knew the primary difference. Either that, or sex was hardwired into his psyche.

She didn't want to think about it. She dove beneath the surface, skimming through the water like a dolphin, trying to outrun the memories. She didn't want to think about sex, or him, or her own uncharacteristic behavior. All she wanted to think about was getting the hell out of there.

Which wasn't going to happen as long as she lurked in the water, unable to face him. She knew

exactly where he was—stretched out under a tree
nearby. Far enough to give her a misleading sense
of privacy, close enough if Mick and Alf came back
this way. Though what he could do to stop them
was beyond her comprehension. They'd have tranquilizer darts, and she knew from bitter experience
just how effective they were. If they managed to
sneak up on John they could knock him out before
he even realized what was happening. And then
she'd be alone, with no one to help.

Except that wasn't going to happen. No one
would sneak up on John without him being aware
of it, she knew that with irrational certainty. And
he wouldn't let anything bad happen to her. Apart,
of course, from what she'd brought on herself.

She swam to the far edge of the lagoon, taking
hold of a root to pull herself out of the water. He
paid no attention, lying perfectly still, and she
moved toward her clothes with undignified haste.

The clothes were almost dry, a blessing. She
pulled them on quickly, then noticed her bra had
disappeared. She hunted the bushes and the trail
leading from the waterfall, but there was no sign of
it. With a muttered curse she pulled the T-shirt over
her naked flesh. In fact it was more comfortable,
but she didn't like the idea of wandering around the
jungle without her bra.

She was being ridiculous. She'd already had sex
with him—what would it matter if he could see her

breasts through the T-shirt? She shoved her hands through her wet hair, sighing as the thick, humid heat settled down around her.

She turned, and John was standing there. She could feel the color rush up her throat, staining her face, and she would have averted her gaze, except that he looked the same as always. Remote, untouchable, barely even aware of her. Apparently those moments in the cave meant absolutely nothing to him.

At least, she could hope so. She tried for a brave smile, but even she could feel it was a little crooked. "I'm sorry. I shouldn't have done that. I feel like an idiot, you know. No, of course, you don't know. Which is just as well—this is embarrassing enough."

She slid her feet into her sandals, then noticed he was coming toward her. She braced herself, wondering if he was fool enough to want sex with her again, and then was momentarily relieved to see he was holding a knife. Her knife, and he was coming right at her.

"What do you think you're doing?" she demanded, her voice wavering in fear. "Granted, the sex wasn't that good, but that doesn't mean you have to…"

He caught her T-shirt in one hand and she let out a little yelp as the knife sliced down. A moment later one sleeve fell off, followed by the second, leaving her arms cool and bare.

"Oh," she said blankly. "Thank you."

He knelt down in front of her, reaching for her pant leg, and she held very still as he ripped the lower half away, so that she was left with shorts. It felt strange, looking down at him from that position, and she wanted to put her hands on his shoulder to steady herself when he pulled the ripped material away from her. She didn't.

And then he was heading off into the rain forest again, obviously expecting her to follow him. She stood there, considering her options. If she went back, Alf would kill her, and Mick would do nothing but watch regretfully. If she struck out on her own she'd probably starve to death or be eaten by wild creatures.

Like it or not, her best chance was with John. He was almost out of sight, and she raced after him, her shame turning into irritation. "You might at least have waited for me," she said. "It's bad enough I jumped you in the cave—you don't have to abandon me for it."

Of course he didn't answer, didn't slow his measured pace, and she trotted along behind him, ignoring the fact that she was more comfortable in her abbreviated clothes, ignoring the fact that his strong, beautiful back was even more distracting than it had been before.

"It's a good thing you don't understand a word I'm saying," she continued, warming to her theme. "That way we don't have to have one of those embarrassing morning-after conversations. Or afternoon-after. Whatever it is I mean. Nothing worse than having to talk to someone you've seen naked. Not that I saw you naked—it was too dark." She was babbling, but it didn't matter. The sound of her voice soothed her, reminded her who and what she was, and couldn't have made any difference to him. At least the sound told him that she was there, trailing after him like a dutiful servant.

"It's no wonder I try to avoid sex altogether," she continued, scrambling over the huge roots that he cleared far more gracefully. "First you have all that stupid seduction crap, where neither of you are sure you want to do it but both of you think you ought to want to. And then there's the act itself, which is usually messy and embarrassing and ultimately unsatisfying. The best that can be said about it is that it means someone wants you, but I'm not sure if that's a price worth paying. And then there's afterward, when you're probably supposed to say you love each other but you'd really much rather be left alone.

"Not that I want to be left alone right now," she added hastily. "And I suppose I'd have to admit that the sex wasn't bad. In fact, it was probably the best I've ever had, and..."

The ever-graceful wild man had managed to stumble for the first time in days, and she barged into him. He caught her before she could fall, and she had the strangest notion that there was an expression in his eyes. Those dark, unfathomable eyes that had held no expression at all.

But when she tried to look for it, it vanished, and he was the same as always. Remote, uncomprehending as he set her away from him and started walking once more.

His hands had disturbed her, of course, but she wasn't sure she wanted to admit that out loud, even to herself. All he'd had to do was touch her and her heart started racing. Though maybe that was just from the strain of keeping up with him.

But no, her heart was racing when they stopped, not when she was scrambling over the jungle landscape to keep up with him.

Maybe she should just stop talking and concentrate on her footing, she thought. It was amazing how much she'd spoken in the last few days. She tended to be a fairly closemouthed person—Richard had complained that she never told him what she was thinking. Which was a good thing, since Richard had tended to take over any original thoughts she'd had. She'd been chattering just about nonstop since they left the house, out of nervousness, out of the sheer, wicked pleasure of being able to say anything she wanted and not have to answer for it.

But she was finally winding down. "I hope you know what you're doing," she said to her companion. "I'm assuming you have some kind of boat stashed around here that will get us off this island without feeding us to the sharks? Which will be fine with me. Actually, after my flight here, I think I'd prefer the sharks to getting in another airplane. I wonder if you've even seen an airplane in your entire life?"

The afternoon shadows were lengthening, and a sudden, horrible thought came to her. What if they had to spend another night on the island? Would he expect to have sex with her again? Would he even want to? And what would she do if he did? Even worse, what would she do if he didn't?

She was so busy worrying about that possible scenario that she failed to notice that the jungle was thinning out. To her astonishment they were coming out of the jungle onto a beach, the greeny-blue Pacific stretching out in front of them in endless, rolling waves.

She glanced up at John, but he seemed unsurprised, so she could only guess that he'd known exactly where he was going. He started down the beach, and she began to follow him, the dutiful little puppy dog, when this time he stopped, turned around and faced her.

She halted, suddenly nervous. He put his hands on her shoulders and pushed her, gently, onto the sand, and she felt a sudden tightening in her stomach, wondering whether he'd want to...whether he thought she'd want to...

But then he moved away, down the beach again, not bothering to look back.

She sat cross-legged on the soft white sand, prepared to wait. She had no idea where he was going, or whether he even intended to come back. For all she knew he'd abandoned her, finally having had enough of her constant chatter.

She rested her chin on her knees, staring at the ever-changing ocean. That was one problem with cities, she had to admit. No ocean, and the broad shores of Lake Michigan didn't even come close. If she hadn't been kidnapped by a wild man, if she weren't running for her life, if her messed-up life suddenly ceased to hassle her, she could be very happy just sitting there, watching the sea slide ever closer to her bare feet. Maybe she wasn't as tied to the city as she'd always thought she was.

She sat, in blissful stillness, as the night began to close in around her. The thought of sleeping with John was beginning to be less frightening and more appealing. They could curl up underneath one of the towering trees like two babes in the woods. Except hadn't the children been found dead in that poem?

And her feelings for John were, unfortunately, far from innocent.

She hadn't even realized he'd come back. One moment she was alone on the beach, the next he was standing beside her. He reached down for her hand and pulled her up, and her heart started pounding with anticipation. Maybe he'd made them a little shelter in the jungle, with a soft, sweet-smelling bed of fronds and flowers, and he'd lead her there and kiss her and...

And she was becoming absolutely revolting, living out some jungle fantasy, she thought in self-disgust. He'd dropped her hand and started back down the beach, and this time she followed, wondering what great delight he'd prepared for her.

They turned onto a little spit of land, and her nervous anticipation vanished in sheer dread.

It was an airplane.

Chapter Eleven

There was no other term for it but blind panic. She tried to run, back down the beach, away from him, but he caught her around the waist, swooping her up and carting her toward the plane. The plane was even smaller than the tiny jet that had brought her to this godforsaken island, and nothing could make her get into it.

Nothing but John, strong and implacable, dragging her there. The back door was open, and he tossed her inside. She hit at him, screaming at him, but it did no good. He was too big, too strong, too invulnerable to anything she might say or do. He caught her wrists in one strong hand, and before she even realized what he was doing, he'd wrapped duct tape around them, efficiently disabling her. He swung her around, wrapped the tape around her ankles with quick efficiency, then ripped off a piece and covered her mouth with it, silencing her shrieks of fury.

He slid the door shut, and she fell back into the darkness, struggling helplessly against the restraints, rage and panic beating against her, so hard that she couldn't catch her breath.

She heard the door open to the cockpit, but she couldn't see anything, hear anything. No voices, just the sound of the motor revving, filling her with even more fear. Who the hell could be flying this tiny little deathtrap?

She wasn't prepared for takeoff. The plane started rolling, tossing her back against something hard, and she hit her head. She tried to struggle to her knees again, but at that moment the plane suddenly took off, into the night sky, and she was thrown back again into a trussed-up heap of utter fear.

This time she stayed where she was, curled up in a fetal position in the darkness, the noise of the plane vibrating all around her. She didn't want to think, didn't want to guess, all she wanted to do was curl up in her misery and retreat into a merciful blankness. Everything in her life had tilted sideways, and she no longer knew what was right and what was wrong. All that she knew was that she'd been tricked.

She must have slept, though she would have considered it an impossibility. Even on big, safe jets she was usually too nervous to sleep, and trussed up in the back of this tiny little plane was hardly conducive to peace of mind. But staying awake with the torrent of thoughts and possibilities running through her brain was an unacceptable alternative, and she gave into the cold and the darkness and the oddly soothing sound of the engines.

She awoke with a start to realize the plane had bumped down into a landing and the engines had been turned off. They were rolling in silence, and she could hear the crackle of brush under the wheels of the plane. And then it stopped, and all was silence and stillness.

She lay there in a curled-up ball, listening to him as he climbed out of the plane, circled it, and came to a stop outside the cargo door. He was in no hurry to open it, and she knew why. Maybe he'd chicken out entirely and just leave her like that for the rest of the night.

She'd underestimated him. As always. The door slid open, but the night was black beyond, only the faint light of the stars overhead.

And John, the wild man, the missing link, the savage with no language and no voice, said, ''Are you ready to calm down?''

It wasn't much of a voice, she had to grant him that. Her initial guess had been right—the rope marks on his neck must have done some damage to his vocal cords, and his voice was rough, harsh, like sandpaper on a block of wood. Laced with an Australian accent.

She would have tried to sit up, but she had real doubts she could manage it without falling over again, and she had already demeaned herself enough in this man's presence. He climbed into the hold of the plane and reached for the duct tape on her mouth.

She hadn't expected gentleness, but the abrupt rip added mortal insult to grievous injury. He pulled her around so that she was sitting and proceeded to cut through the tape on her ankles, then on her wrists. With the Swiss Army knife he'd taken from her.

It was the final straw. She yanked her arms apart so that the cut duct tape fell on her lap, and she slapped him full across the face, as hard as she could.

It was a lot harder than she'd realized. Her hand was numb from the force, and his head whipped back in shock. He was still holding the knife, and she belatedly realized that might not have been the smartest thing she'd ever done, given that she knew absolutely nothing about him except that he was a cheat and a liar. But she didn't care.

"All right," he said finally. "I guess I owe you that one. But don't try it again. I've had my fill of being hit in the last few months and I'm not about to put up with any more of it."

She opened her mouth to say something, then closed it again. She was, quite simply, speechless, with fury and embarrassment. He'd understood everything she'd been saying. About Richard, about her family, about her sex life…oh, God, about him. She'd blithely told him she lusted after him. Blithely told him the sex had been the best she ever had.

She clamped her mouth shut, glaring at him, keeping her hands folded in her lap so she wouldn't hit him again. She was still reeling in shock from so many things, not the least was the fact that she'd actually hit another human being when she prided herself on her self-control. She'd slapped him so hard her hand still hurt, and she actually wanted to hit him again.

The only way she was going to get through this was to retreat inside herself until she was calm enough to handle it. And him. She glared at him.

He was totally unmoved by her rage, but that was nothing new. He'd been totally unmoved by everything she'd said or done, with the minor exception of sex. And she certainly wasn't going to be thinking about that again—this was horrendous enough without that ludicrous distraction. She waited with deceptive patience as he climbed back out of the plane, and he held out a hand to help her down.

She ignored it, sliding forward on her butt and swinging her legs over the side of the cargo hold. They were in the middle of an open field, with the stars all around, and she knew a moment's desperate hope that he'd brought her back to civilization.

No such luck. The night was dark, lit only by the stars. No blessed light pollution, nothing but Mother Nature to guide their way.

The ground was soft and spongy beneath her feet, and her knees were cramped from the uncomfortable ride in the back of the airplane, but she didn't even flinch. The last thing she needed to do was collapse at his feet, give him a reason to touch her. Not that he seemed the slightest bit interested in touching her.

"Follow me," he said, heading toward the edge of the clearing and a wide path. She stayed where she was, considering her alternatives. He stopped, looking back at her.

"This is another island, and there's no one around who can help you. I'd suggest you sleep in the plane, but I'm thinking you'll be wanting a bed after the last two days. My place is just down the road. And don't give me that look—there's a guest room. You can sleep in pristine privacy."

He was a sarcastic son of a bitch, she thought grimly. She liked him better when he couldn't talk. He was right, though—she didn't have much choice. At that point she was willing to trade her pride for a bed, as long as it was a single one.

Once more she was following his strong, beautiful back through a jungle. This time, however, the track was wide, built for a car. This time she knew he wasn't a beautiful, untamed creature. He was a lying pig who'd taken advantage of her gullibility.

She would have given ten years off her life if they hadn't had sex. It was that simple—she could have handled the embarrassment, the betrayal, anything, if she just hadn't...if he just hadn't...

She had to stop thinking about it. She couldn't change the past, and right now she was stuck in a completely humiliating present. It wouldn't last that long. He had to be as eager to get rid of her as she was to leave—he'd get her off the island by tomorrow and she'd never have to see him or think of him again.

Except when she dealt with the remnants of her career. She'd destroyed it for his sake, and she tried to summon up outrage. She couldn't. He'd been trapped, drugged, tortured by Hunnicutt's minions, and if they'd found out he wasn't their golden jungle child they probably would have killed him. No, she couldn't regret what she'd done, no matter how high the price.

She just wished she'd kept her big mouth shut. Among other things.

It was less than five minutes to their destination, but Libby would have been happy if it had taken five hours. She was totally unprepared for the small villa-type house sitting on a wide stretch of beach. It looked like a typical tropical bungalow—porches running the length of the house, lots of windows to let in the breeze.

He started up the front steps, and she held back, contemplating returning to the empty plane. He pushed open the front door, then turned back to her. "Coming?"

She wasn't going to dignify that with an answer. She followed him up the wide front steps, slowly, reluctantly, half expecting some angry owner to appear with a shotgun. He'd called it his place, but she didn't believe him. She didn't believe a word he said.

No angry owner appeared, of course. The front porch opened onto one big room, and she stood there while John, or whoever he was, moved through the house, lighting candles and kerosene lamps so that the place was slowly illuminated. He disappeared into one of the back rooms, and she moved toward a wicker chair, sitting down on it with a weary sigh.

It was too dark to make out any of the details of the room. There were walls of books, which presumably her wild man had read. There were shabby, comfortable chairs, but no sign of a telephone. There was a desk, covered with neatly piled papers, as if someone who wasn't naturally tidy had tried to put it in order, and she was half tempted to go over and see if she could find any answers in those stacks of papers. She stayed put.

He appeared out of the darkness with his usual graceful stealth, but she'd been listening for him and managed to control her instinctive shriek. If she could manage it, he wasn't even going to hear her breathe.

"I've turned on the fridge and the hot water. They're both run by gas, and it shouldn't be long before one's cold and one's hot. I've got a generator, but it's a pain in the ass to turn it on in the dark. It's only got enough juice to run a few lights, anyway, so we can make do with candles. And since you're so curious, yes, this is my house. This is where I live when megalomaniac billionaires don't keep me tied up and drugged."

She wasn't as good as he had been at keeping an impassive expression on her face, but she was making a halfway decent attempt. Enough to annoy him, which was reward enough.

"Tomorrow we'll find a way to get you off-island. In the meantime you might as well make the best of it. Feel free to tell me what a bastard I am. I'm expecting it."

Lord, it was tempting. But there weren't enough words to tell him exactly what she was feeling, and besides, silence seemed so much more effective.

For the first time she actually saw an emotion cross his usually impassive face. Even in the shadowed room she could recognize the sheer frustration, and she suppressed a satisfied smile.

"First you don't stop talking, then you don't start," he said bitterly. "Anyone ever tell you that you were a woman of extremes?"

He could certainly play rougher than that, and she wondered idly whether he would or not. She'd said so many revealing things to him when she thought he wouldn't understand that he could easily turn around and use them to goad her. She wasn't going to let them get to her. But she was interested to see what he'd use for a weapon. She already knew he could be absolutely ruthless when he wanted to be—the marks on her wrist were still there.

He turned on his heel, leaving the room, and she let a small, secret smile cross her face. Score one for the good guys, she thought. And then she remembered the observation room, the man lying drugged and helpless on a camouflage gurney, with Mick and Alf poking at him. And she'd been one of them. Maybe she wasn't one of the good guys after all.

He was back, sooner than she expected, with a pile of clothes and a towel in his hands. He dropped them in her lap. "These will have to do. You could try the shower now—the water's been preheated by the cistern, and if you don't mind it lukewarm…"

She rose and pushed past him, not even hesitating. She found the bathroom just off the kitchen, and she slammed the door behind her, in his face.

''You could at least thank me for letting you take the first shower,'' he called out through the door. ''You've had one a lot more recently than I have.''

Poor baby, she thought with a total lack of sympathy. She had every intention of taking as long as she possibly could. In a climate like this the water probably never ran cold, but she'd use up every bit of warmth she could.

She almost wept with pleasure at the first touch of the shower on her body. He had sandalwood soap and real shampoo, and she scrubbed every inch of her scalp and her skin, rinsed, and scrubbed again. Her legs were scratched from walking through the undergrowth, her wrist was still bruised. And then she looked down at her body. To her absolute horror she could see the imprint of his fingers on her hips, and she knew where that had come from.

She'd always bruised far too easily. If she'd hoped to wash all memory of that afternoon from her body, it was easier said than done. Some things wouldn't go with soap and scrubbing. Including her memories and emotions.

She heard him pounding on the door. ''Are you going to take all night?''

She considered it. It would annoy him, which was a blessing, but it would only put off the inevitable. Once she emerged he'd take his own shower, and she could find her bedroom and lock herself in and he wouldn't bother her again. Tomorrow, in the light of day, maybe she'd bring herself to talk to him. Just a clipped sentence or two to tell him where she wanted to go. And where she wanted him to go, for that matter.

But for tonight, she was mum. Not one syllable was he getting from her. He'd had more than enough to last him—he should cherish the silence.

She kept the shower running from sheer malice when she finally stepped out into the steamy bathroom. Rubbing the mist off the mirror, she looked at her reflection. She was sunburned, of course, and her short hair was wild, curling around her face. Unfortunately she didn't look like the dignified, wounded ice princess. She looked rosy-cheeked and hurt and nauseatingly wholesome.

Not that he'd even notice.

He'd brought her some of his own clothes. Considering he was more than a foot taller than she was, the fit was far from ideal, but she didn't really care. No underwear, and she wondered whether he wore any. A pair of khaki shorts that sank to her hips and just barely stayed there and a T-shirt so huge it almost covered the shorts. She pulled up the shirt, staring at her body. The shorts hung low enough that she could see his handprints on her hips. It was a small consolation that she'd be the only one to know they were there. After all, she was the only one who would care.

The water was nice and cool when she reached over to turn it off, and she allowed herself one last wicked smile before replacing it with a somber, enigmatic expression worthy of the wild man himself.

He was sitting at the kitchen table when she finally emerged. He'd lit an oil lamp, and there was a plate of food waiting for her. Probably poisoned.

Unfortunately she was hungry enough to eat poison. "I went ahead and ate without you, since you seemed determined to take your sweet time," he said. "Any hot water left?"

She took a seat at the table, ignoring him. Canned peaches, tuna fish and crackers. It was all she could do not to fall on it like a starving orphan.

She schooled herself to wait. He rose, making an annoyed growl, and headed for the bathroom. "Don't think you can keep this up, Libby," he warned her. "When I get out of the shower you and I are going to have a long talk, whether you like it or not. You hear me?"

She picked up her fork and began to eat, studiously ignoring him. He slammed the bathroom door behind him.

It didn't take long to finish what was on her plate, and then she went scouting for more. Only warm beer in the slowly chilling refrigerator—what else would she expect? More cans of soup and fruit on the shelves, plus dried pasta, sauce and various nonperishables. She found a slightly ancient candy bar, ate that, and then wandered through the rest of the small house.

He hadn't lied—there was a guest room where she could safely barricade herself inside. Not that she had any illusions about her own desirability. Clearly her wild man would take what was practically forced on him, but he wouldn't have to settle for...for...

She wasn't going to let her mind go in that direction. The guest room was small, Spartan, with a narrow iron bed and a sagging mattress and a mosquito net overhead. Even that would be better than sleeping on the ground. Wrapped in his arms. Safe. Protected.

Stop it! It's over. Tomorrow you'll never have to see him again.

At the back of the house lay his bedroom. She assumed the French doors led out to a lanai off the back, but she wasn't about to take one step inside the portal to see. There was a bed, a big one, with mosquito netting, a chest of drawers, a table and some chairs. There were books piled everywhere—on the bedside table, on the floor, on the dresser, but not much else.

The only other room in the place was a small study. More books, another desk, a laptop computer. At the sight of the computer Libby felt a rush of absolute grief. She'd left hers behind, without a second thought, the top-of-the-line computer she loved more than anything. And she hadn't even thought twice about it.

It was one thing stepping into his bedroom, another into his study. She walked to the desk, checking to see whether there was a modem cord, when she had an unpleasant shock. He had the same computer she had.

It might not have the same bells and whistles, but it was still essentially the same model. She ought to claim it as recompense for saving his life, except, of course, that he'd saved hers in return. And it was bad enough to be wearing his clothes. Using his computer would be much more intimate.

She realized the shower was no longer running. But she was. She wasn't ready for a confrontation. She was tired and emotional and nowhere certain she could manage to keep her icy demeanor if he really pushed her. Sooner or later she'd have to deal with him, she knew that. But she needed time, and space, before she was ready to do that. In the meantime, retreat was the best defense.

She closed her bedroom door behind her, shoved a chair under the doorknob and climbed into bed. The springs creaked beneath her weight, and the night air was beginning to cool off. She could hear him moving around out in the kitchen, and she held her breath.

She half expected him to pound on her door, to shake the doorknob, to demand that she come out and talk to him. She would have enjoyed answering him with potent silence.

But he didn't. The various noises in the household began to fade away, and soon there was no sound but the singing of the night birds outside.

Libby leaned over and blew out the candle beside her bed. And then she pulled the sheet over her, curled up into a little ball, and thanked heaven she was all alone in this narrow, uncomfortable bed.

Chapter Twelve

Considering that he was finally back home, back in a place he thought he might never see again, John ought to have been in a better mood. He stretched out on his bed, the first real bed he'd slept on since he could remember, and told himself he was just restless. He needed privacy, and until he got rid of Libby Holden he was bound to feel on edge.

After all, he hadn't had a moment's peace in God knows how long. On impulse he got out of bed and crossed the bedroom in the dark. He hadn't taken his watch when he'd gone on his walkabout, but the battery was probably still working. He could find out the date.

He found it in the top drawer, pushed the button that illuminated the face and stared at it in disbelief. January 16. He'd flown over to Ghost Island on October 1. He'd been held for almost three months.

He dropped the watch back on the dresser, taking

a deep, calming breath. Three months of his life had vanished into a drug- and pain-riddled haze. The question was, what was he going to do about it?

And of more immediate importance, what was he going to do about his unwilling guest? In fact, he'd kidnapped her twice. Not that he'd had any choice in the matter—it had been sheer instinct that made him grab her in the first place, but by the time they got to the plane he'd known there was no safety left for her anywhere near Hunnicutt's goons.

So he had her. What the hell was he going to do with her? His jaw still ached from the sock she'd given him—she was stronger than he'd realized. But then, she'd managed to keep up with him through the grueling trek, even scared and angry and embarrassed. She was a hell of a lot more resilient and resourceful than he would have thought a city woman should be.

He'd been hoping she would have calmed down by the time she'd had a shower and eaten. He hadn't even complained about the total lack of hot water—if tiny acts of revenge helped her salvage her pride then he'd put up with it.

But she'd already gone to bed when he'd emerged, hiding from him, and he hadn't had the energy to battle it. Tomorrow would be soon enough to sort things out.

Or so he'd thought, but now here it was hours

later and he couldn't sleep. He kept thinking about her. About her annoying, endless chatter. About her infuriating silence. About her small, still body beneath his. And about how she said that pitifully inadequate sex act had been the best sex she'd ever had.

He threw himself back on the bed, furious with himself. He used to have more self-discipline than that. He needed sleep, and he'd always been able to simply will it to come. If something was distracting him he'd never had any problem dismissing it from his mind.

But Libby refused to be dismissed. She was haunting him, the dazed, vulnerable look on her face when he'd kissed her, the ridiculous bravado after they'd made love. Her fear when she'd heard Alf's plans, her fierce rage when he spoke to her. Emotions rioting through her, so many of them that he felt stunned.

He definitely needed to get rid of her, and fast. She was already disrupting his life far too effectively, and he was desperate to have his old life back.

He threw himself back on the bed, running a hand through his long hair. At least it was clean, untangled. His face was clean-shaven as well, and he wondered how she'd react when she saw him. Probably with complete disdain.

She liked her wild man. How would she like one who was marginally civilized?

The noise woke him. It was the middle of the night, but he was acutely sensitive to the sounds around him, and he heard the scrape of the chair, the faint creak as the guest room door opened, the soft sound of her footsteps. He held his breath, then released it in profound disappointment. She wasn't coming to his bedroom, she was heading for the living room.

Was she fool enough to try to leave? He wouldn't put it past her, and he certainly couldn't just turn over and try to reclaim sleep without making sure she wasn't going any farther than the living room.

The sound of the front door galvanized him out of bed, and he was out there in seconds, ready to haul her back, looking forward to an excuse to touch her. Because he knew what would happen when he did.

No such luck, though. She'd opened the door, all right, but she hadn't gone out. She was sitting at the desk, a candle lit against the darkness, staring down at something.

"I thought you were trying to sneak out," he said.

She must have heard his approach. She didn't turn, ignoring him as she stared at the thing in her hand. Belatedly he recognized it, and he felt the familiar defenses closing down around him. He al-

most turned around and went back to his bedroom,
rather than answer her questions.

But she had no questions. She wouldn't speak to
him, and it was making him absolutely crazy. He'd
do anything to get her to acknowledge his existence, anything.

"That's a picture of my family," he said in the
raw voice he was slowly becoming used to. He
wondered if he'd ever regain his normal, deep
voice, or whether it would always sound like gravel
in a blender. "The last one taken."

She didn't react, but she still held the frame,
looking down at it rather than back at him. He knew
the portrait so well—his aunt had given it to him
when he was seventeen. When he'd come back.

"We were supposed to be flying to Hawaii, making stops along the way. My father was a pilot, a
damned good one, and he didn't trust flying with
anyone else.

"My mother was a botanist with the University
of Sydney, my father was a geologist, and I was
their only child. We traveled everywhere together,
until that last flight.

"We crashed. A storm came up, out of the blue,
and we went down in a cove off Ghost Island. My
parents died, I didn't. I was eight years old."

She still didn't turn. But she didn't let go of the
picture. "I'd been a normal kid up till then. Maybe
a little more traveled than most, but I liked the usual

things. Sports and television and rock and roll. I wasn't really prepared for Ghost Island.

"I buried my parents," he said without emotion. "And I lived alone on that island for nine years. I don't know how I managed to survive, but I did, until stories began to circulate, and someone actually came looking for me. They brought me back to my aunt, my only living relative, and I was a national hero. The Wild Child, who'd survived in an Australian rain forest for nine years on his own."

She set the photograph down, but she still didn't move. He didn't know whether he was reaching her or not, didn't know what he really expected from her.

"I tried to make it back in civilization. I had lots of money—the insurance company had paid off on my parents' deaths and my aunt hadn't touched a penny of it. They'd paid handsomely for the death of their eight-year-old son, but once they found out I was alive they weren't in any hurry to ask for it back. I guess the insurance company figured they'd be liable for a lot more, given my time on the island. They were the ones who'd had us all declared dead and the search for the missing plane called off."

He moved into the room, closer to her. Her hair was a riot of unruly curls around her head, and he started to think maybe he liked short hair on women after all. At least, he liked it on Libby.

"I was what they called gifted. I finished my basic schooling in two years flat, went to university and decided to be a botanist like my mother. After all, if there was one thing I knew, it was plant life— I'd lived off it, slept under it, worn it for more than half my life. But I couldn't do it. After six months in the city something snapped, and I took off. I bought this place, where I'm left alone, the way I like it. I go back to the city every year and teach a course or two, but mostly I live here and do research. And then I go off into the wilderness, for weeks, months on end. I think I'd go crazy if I had to be around other people without any break."

He came up behind her. He could smell the scent of his soap on her skin, see her small, fragile shoulders beneath his T-shirt, and it gave him a strangely possessive feeling. Strange, because he'd tried never to possess anything in his life.

"And my name really is John. John Bartholomew Hunter. Better known as Hunter by the few people who can put up with me long enough to become friends. Tarzan to my enemies."

Even that didn't get a response from her. She pushed away from the table, and he stepped back so she wouldn't bump into him. He was a man who lived by his instincts, and his instincts told him it wasn't going to be tonight. She had too many things to work through.

"I don't know why I'm bothering to tell you this since you obviously couldn't care less, but I figured I owe it to you. I'll see about getting you home as soon as I can. In the meantime, don't you think you could at least say something? At least look at me?"

Obviously not. She rose, blew out the candle, plunging the room into darkness. And with better night vision than he would have given her credit for, she skirted him, went back to her room and closed the door behind her. The sound of the chair being wedged beneath the doorknob brought a faint, bitter smile to his face.

So much for mending fences. What had he expected, that she'd weep over his childhood? He hadn't wept over it—hadn't wept over anything since he'd buried his parents twenty-five years ago.

Which reminded him. Hunnicutt had the absolute gall to have bought the deserted island for his little experiments. He'd bought his parents' resting place, and even if John had felt any urge to forgive and forget his incarceration, he wasn't going to ignore that. As soon as he got rid of Libby he could concentrate on making Hunnicutt pay a suitable recompense.

He'd do everything he could to get her off-island by tomorrow. There was only one small, bitter problem with that.

He didn't want her to go.

LIBBY WAS AMAZED she'd slept so well. It had to be late morning—the sun was streaming in the windows of her small room, and all was still and quiet.

She really didn't want to leave the safety of the bedroom. She wasn't ready to face him... John...again. But she was starving, restless and unable to stay in bed a moment longer, and she steeled herself to deal with him. Just because she had to see him didn't mean she had to talk to him.

She moved the chair and flung open the door defiantly. All for nothing. The kitchen was deserted. And so, her instincts told her, was the house.

She didn't find the note until after she'd taken another long, blissful shower and stolen another set of his clothes. The marks on her hips had faded, but her wrist was still sore and bruised. Maybe she'd get over him when the bruises disappeared. Maybe not.

He'd left the note by the picture of the young boy and his parents, the picture that had haunted her dreams. "Gone up island to see about getting you a way out of here. Be back tonight. John."

She crumpled up the piece of paper and tossed it in the trash. And then for some reason she picked it out again, smoothing the wrinkles. Foolishness on her part—she was going to be out of there before long, and she shouldn't need anything to remember him by. But she tucked it in the pocket of her shorts, anyway.

She was starving enough to try making scrambled eggs out of powdered egg and powdered milk on the gas stove. The results were surprisingly good. No Tab, of course, and at the moment she would have killed for any kind of pop, even an orange soda. She made do with coffee, taking a large mug of it out onto the front veranda.

She dragged a wicker rocker over to the wide railing, propped her feet up and stared out at the ocean, cradling the coffee on her stomach. The sound of the waves was incredibly soothing, the wind rustled the palm trees overhead, and in the distance she could hear the cry of birds. She had probably never been anywhere so remote in her entire life.

She should be anxious, restless, desperate to get back to people and civilization. Though she wasn't quite sure why. What people? She had friends, but mostly they'd been Richard's friends, not hers. The women she knew were either humorless workaholics or giddy airheads.

She missed her family. She had that much in common with John—they were both alone in this world, no families left. But that was about all.

She tilted her chair back, staring at the horizon. They must be somewhere near the Great Barrier Reef if she remembered her Australian geography, which was questionable. There was no denying that the climate here was perfect, the scenery gorgeous, the air heavenly. If she were to live here she wouldn't have nearly so Spartan an existence. She'd have electricity and a satellite dish for telephone and television and Internet connections. She'd have a much better variety of food, a less-intimidating library, and a fireplace for rainy days.

The place could use a pantry, full of useful stores. A decent stereo would help matters as well. And closets—the house had no decent closets, and the sheets on her bed were practically threadbare. Something light, cotton, with flowers on it...

She sloshed some of the hot coffee on her stomach, staining his T-shirt as she sat up abruptly. What the hell was she doing, planning her future? There was no future for her in a place like this, with a man like him. Even if he wanted her, which he obviously didn't, she'd have to want him as well, which was outside the realm of possibility. So the sex had been...quite nice. Obviously she'd chosen poorly in the past. Next time she wouldn't settle for messy and undignified. Next time she'd see if she could find a partner who could make her feel things. A partner like John.

She slammed her feet on the porch. "Idiot," she said aloud, knowing he wasn't anywhere near to hear her voice. "Stupid, sentimental, irrational, romantic, impractical idiot. The sooner you get out of here, the better."

There was no one there to disagree, only a small, insistent voice in her head, and she'd learned long ago to ignore it.

She looked out at the waves rolling gently onto the shore. It was incredibly soothing, just sitting there watching the ocean. She could have sat there forever, for weeks, for months, for years. She could have sat there forever. With him.

She might as well accept the fact that she'd been avoiding for the last twelve hours. Hell, she'd been avoiding it for longer than that, but those days didn't count. She hadn't even known what she was up against.

The bottom line was, she didn't want to go. Didn't want to leave him, didn't want to leave this place. She wanted to go into the back of the house, take off all her clothes and climb into his big bed. She had the most insane desire to start cleaning, rearranging things, when she'd never been much of a nester in her entire life. She wanted this place, and this man, and she wasn't going to have, either. So she sat on the lanai, staring at the ocean, and let herself cry.

Times like these called for desperate measures, she thought when her first fit of weeping had passed. Times like these called for chocolate.

The bastard had none, only that elderly candy bar that she'd consumed the night before. Oh, sure, he had more than a case of beer, but the closest thing to chocolate was an old tin of baker's cocoa. She was desperate enough to try a spoonful, but she spat it out, shuddering. It was unsweetened.

It took her ages to realize what she did have. Dried eggs and oil and flour and sugar. All the things she needed to make brownies. John didn't have anything useful like a cookbook among all his learned tomes on botany, but the blessed tin had a recipe on the back. No measuring cups, either, but she simply guessed. She almost gave up when she was ready to put the pan into the oven and discovered that the damned thing didn't have an automatic pilot, and she considered sitting on the porch and eating the batter plain. But she was made of sterner stuff than that, and if brownies weren't worth risking life and limb for, then what was?

To her amazement the oven lit easily enough, with only one terrifying pop. She'd had to fashion a brownie pan out of several thick layers of tinfoil, and she slid it into the oven, keeping her fingers crossed. If they worked, she'd survive. Brownies made anything bearable.

She almost started crying again when the brownies came out. They were perfect—soft and chewy, and she ate half the pan, burning her mouth as she did it, letting the blissful chocolate waves wash over her. As long as there was chocolate in the world things could never be too bad.

She was half tempted to hide the rest of the chocolate in her room—he didn't deserve to share her body or her chocolate, but she decided that would be too petty. Instead she decided to snoop, wandering through the place, trying to figure out what kind of man John Bartholomew Hunter really was. It was growing dark when she struck gold. A small hardcover book, clearly written for older children, was tucked sideways in one of the bookshelves. A gangly teenager with familiar eyes stared out from the cover, and the title, *Wild Child,* told the rest. The book was copyrighted fourteen years ago, but that didn't matter. It was his past that interested her. She already knew the present.

She took one of the oil lamps back to her room, curled up on the bed and started to read. She was so engrossed she didn't hear the front door open, didn't hear the footsteps in the kitchen.

It was only when a shadow darkened her door that she looked up, startled, at the strange man standing there, watching her.

And then she realized it was John.

Chapter Thirteen

He'd shaved. His jaw was smooth, tanned, un-
adorned by the rough beard. His hair was too long,
pushed back from his face, but it was smooth and
silky, not the tangled mat that it had been. He wore
the same clothes she did, the only clothes he
seemed to own—khaki shorts and a white T-shirt,
and for some reason the sight of him in a shirt,
when she was so accustomed to him wearing so
little, was even more disturbing.

She looked into his face, schooling her own expression into one of utter disinterest. It was rough
going. He had the face of an angel. No, the face of
a fallen angel, high cheekbones, a strong jaw, a
rich, generous mouth. And his eyes, his deep brown
liquid eyes, no longer shuttered and opaque, watching her, expecting something from her. Something
she wasn't willing to give.

"Don't tell me the shock of my appearance isn't

enough to make you speak?'' he said, the irony clear in his raspy voice.

She wanted to turn her back on him, turn to the book, but she couldn't. For one thing, she couldn't quite bring herself not to look at him. He was like chocolate for the eyes, and she was having a hard time resisting, at least the looking part.

And she didn't particularly want him to see what she was reading. She didn't want to give him the satisfaction of knowing how curious she was about his past. She already knew he was older than she'd thought, thirty-three years old. She knew things she hadn't wanted to know—about the little boy alone on an uninhabited island, trying to survive, and part of her wanted to jump up and put her arms around him, to put his head on her breast and stroke his face.

But that wasn't what she really wanted, and she knew it.

And it certainly wasn't what he wanted. He just wanted her gone, and his blessed privacy back again. Nothing personal, of course. He'd learned to live without people and he preferred it that way.

''There's a boat coming for you tomorrow morning that'll take you to the mainland. The captain's an old friend of mine, and he'll see to it you get your passport replaced and get a ticket home. Unless you were wanting to go back and talk to Hunnicutt.''

She turned her back at that, carefully shielding the book from his gaze.

"I thought not. The captain will be here mid-morning, so you won't have to put up with these primitive conditions for too much longer. Once I deal with Hunnicutt I'll see about getting your belongings shipped back to you in the States. I assume he'll have your address."

That almost got her, but she kept her gaze on the wall. Deal with Hunnicutt? What did he think he would accomplish against someone with Hunnicutt's billions? That kind of money could buy any kind of protection—he'd be helpless.

It wasn't her concern, she reminded herself sternly. Even if she were disposed to talk, he wouldn't listen. She'd gotten him out of that mess, and he'd returned the favor. They were even. If he chose to walk straight back into the lion's den again, then it was out of her hands.

"You know," he said casually, "you'd make one hell of a wife. You've got the silent treatment down pat—it's almost as effective as the Chinese water torture. If I had to choose between some of the little electric experiments that first doctor was practicing on me and your class-A snit, I think I'd prefer the electricity."

That made her turn. The word *wife* was a lot more shocking than anything else he could have said, and he seemed to realize it. He took a step back, a physical distancing, but she didn't move, watching him out of calm, steady eyes.

"I'll make dinner," he said. "But just so you don't have any more nasty surprises, I thought I better mention something. My mother was French."

She stared at him stonily, and then, just as he turned away, the other shoe dropped. She'd chattered away at him in French, using that language for her most embarrassing confessions. And he'd understood every word.

She rolled on her stomach, barely managing to stifle her moan of sheer mortification. She'd thought things could only improve. She was wrong.

He made spaghetti. She could smell the tomato sauce wafting through the house on the tropical breezes, and her stomach growled. No one could ruin spaghetti, and she was absolutely starving.

One more night to get through, she reminded herself. One more night, curled up in this concave bed, and then she'd be out of here. She didn't really need to eat dinner—she'd gone longer without eating. So she was starving. There were worse things in the world. Like trying to ignore John while she ate.

"Dinner's ready."

Well, maybe starving wasn't as easy as she thought. Besides, there was still half a tray of brownies left and her chocolate cravings had barely been touched. Tucking the book under the covers, she climbed out of bed and headed into the kitchen.

He was standing at the counter, watching her. She still couldn't get used to his face, his hair. If she'd had any sense she should have found him less attractive. She couldn't see any sign of the wild man who'd carried her off into the jungle, saved her life, protected her, and she missed him.

But not as much as she was going to miss John Hunter when the boat carried her away the next morning.

"I was going to set the table on the porch, but I figured you wouldn't want to sit with me, so I served you a plate and you can take it somewhere and eat it in private. Since I cooked you get to do the dishes, but I'm not holding my breath."

She kept her gaze averted, picking up one of the plates of spaghetti and the fork he'd set out. She glanced around for the brownies, far more interested in them, but they'd disappeared from their place on the counter.

It was enough to make her look at him. His smile was calmly infuriating. "Nice of you to make dessert," he observed. "I didn't know it was possible to make brownies out of the stuff I had kicking around here. Now all you have to do is ask me where they are and I'll tell you."

Kidnapping was one thing. The bruises on her wrist were another. Lies, treachery and deceit were more nails in the coffin. But there was nothing, absolutely nothing worse than separating a woman from her chocolate. She gave him a glare that would have frozen hell.

He shrugged, singularly unmoved by her silent fury. "You'll have to do better than that, Libby. Ask me where the brownies are, or do without."

She was, after all, a lady. She didn't hurl the plate of spaghetti at his head, no matter how much she wanted to. She simply set it down on the counter, untouched, and went out to the front porch, closing the door behind her.

He didn't make the mistake of coming after her, and she didn't waste her time going back in. She wasn't going to cry over lost brownies or abandoned spaghetti, and she certainly wasn't going to cry over leaving this remote, abandoned, empty, derelict, ill-kept, utterly serene piece of paradise.

And most of all, she wasn't going to cry about walking away from her wild man. He'd disappeared into the mists, leaving a stranger behind. A stranger who frightened her even more than the savage.

There was a thin sliver of moon hanging low over the ocean, and the stars were out in force. She put her feet up on the railing, watching as the tide receded and the evening air grew cool around her. She had to make it through one more night without falling apart. Once she got back to Chicago she could go into a Victorian decline and not come out of it for months. For now she had to tough it out.

She'd left her watch behind at Ghost Island, so

she had no idea what time it was. She'd left everything behind, including her common sense, and she
hadn't even thought of it. But he had. She was in
the middle of nowhere, no clothes, no identification,
no money, no passport, thanks to him. No, that
wasn't true. It had been her choice to free him. She
just hadn't realized how much she'd be giving up.
Her career was one thing. Her computer, her cell
phone and her peace of mind made it a different
situation altogether.

The door to his bedroom was closed, and one
lone oil lamp stood burning on the kitchen counter.
The food had been put away, and she wondered
whether there'd be cold spaghetti in the fridge. It
might be worth a try.

At least she wouldn't have to see him again. She
wouldn't have to be tempted again by…

His door opened, and he stood there, filling it,
still in his shorts and T-shirt, holding the tinfoil pan
of brownies in one hand. "Looking for these?" he
asked in as dulcet a tone as his ruined voice could
manage.

It was the last straw. She grabbed for them, but
he moved them out of reach, deftly, and she followed, in a blind fury, into his room, not even re-
alizing where she was until he kicked the door shut
behind her.

"That's better," he said calmly. "And now you

and I are going to have a talk, whether you like it or not.''

She spun around, ready to run, but he caught her, his hand closing around her bruised wrist, and she let out an involuntary yelp of pain, shocking him.

''What's wrong?'' he demanded, releasing her wrist but catching her elbow so she couldn't escape. He looked down at the marks on her wrist, and a second later he released her, horrified. ''I didn't do that,'' he said flatly.

She didn't say anything. She didn't have a clear shot to the door, but it was close. If she just held still long enough to allay his suspicions, she could make a run for it.

She wasn't afraid of him. Not afraid that he would deliberately hurt her. Just afraid that she wouldn't be able to fight him anymore. That she'd start yelling at him, and if she did she'd start crying, and she didn't think she could stand it.

''Those are old bruises,'' he said. ''Did Alf do that to you? Mick?''

She said nothing. She didn't need to. He looked at her and knew the truth, and he began to curse, foul, colorful obscenities directed at himself. ''I didn't know, Libby,'' he said. ''It must have been when they shot me so full of drugs. I didn't realize. No wonder you're frightened of me.''

She couldn't very well tell him otherwise. She

simply nodded and started for the door, grateful for the easy escape.

Unfortunately he got there ahead of her, and she realized her relief was premature. He leaned up against the door, blocking her way, and she halted. Why did he have to be so big, she thought desperately, and why did she have to be so damned short? It wasn't that his size was particularly menacing, at least not anymore. But it was…distracting. Disturbing.

"But that doesn't explain why you'd have sex with me after I did that to you. And I'm not going to start believing anything kinky, like you're into pain—I know that's not true. So you obviously forgave me for hurting you. But you're not about to forgive me now, are you?"

In fact, she couldn't forgive him when he hadn't even said he was sorry, but she wasn't about to point that out to him. She just waited for him to move, certain that he'd have to, sooner or later. She could be just as stubborn as he was, and the longer this went on, the more determined she was not to speak.

"So while we're having this heart-to-heart chat, Libby," he continued, "why don't you explain to me why some of the lousiest sex in my life was the best you ever had?"

It was so unexpectedly cruel that her defenses were ripped away, so cruel that words, which should have come then, failed her. She looked up at him in stunned shock, and realized that her eyes were stinging. *Oh, God, don't let me cry in front of him,* she begged. *I'll do anything, anything, just don't let me cry.*

It was small comfort that he looked equally horrified. "I didn't mean that," he said quickly. "Not that way. I meant...oh, for God's sake!"

She was crying now, and she wasn't going to stand in front of him and let him watch. She charged him like a bull, trying to move him out of the way of the door, but she might as well have been a mosquito dive-bombing a bear. He could hold her off one-handed.

"Cut it out, Libby! I just meant you must have had a lousy time. I still can't figure out why you wanted to do it when you wouldn't even let me touch you. Ouch!" She kicked him, hard, though she stubbed her toes doing it. She considered kneeing him in the balls, but he was too tall for her to reach, so she punched him in the stomach.

"You're a violent little thing when you're pissed off, aren't you?" he said calmly. "So instead of hitting me, why don't you just tell me how you were able to enjoy sex when it was over just as you were getting turned on? Or has it just been so long since you've been laid that anything would do? Because trust me, I can do a much better job than that given the right time and place. Like now."

She stopped hitting him, as real panic washed over her. He was holding her arms, carefully, so he wouldn't hurt her, but enough to keep her from doing any real damage. Enough to keep her from running away. She looked up at him, not bothering to disguise her panic.

"It's very simple, Libby. Tell me no. That's all you have to do. Just say no. Because if you're not going to, I'm going to take you over to that bed and show you what the best sex in your life ought to be. And that's a promise."

She couldn't get her mouth to work. Her voice had caught in her throat, and there was no way she could bring the word out that she needed.

He waited, patiently, and then he nodded, a faint, satisfied smile on his face. "Nothing to say? Good. Get on the bed."

He caught her elbow before it landed in his stomach, turned her around and picked her up, carrying her over to the bed and dropping her in the middle of it. He pulled his shirt over his head, tossed it on the floor, and suddenly he looked like John again. Clean-shaven, long-haired, wild and dangerous, he looked like the creature she'd seen trapped in that phony jungle room.

Say something, she told herself urgently. *He'll listen. He said he would. Tell him no.* But she kept her mouth shut, silent, as he climbed onto the big high bed, crawling toward her like a sleek, dangerous jungle cat.

He reached for the hem of her T-shirt, and she didn't stop him as he pulled it over her head, tossing it after his, exposing her breasts. He sat back and looked at her in the flickering candlelight, and she wanted to cover herself with her hands. She didn't. She just sat there, defiant, waiting. Waiting for him to change his mind? Waiting for him to do what he promised? She wasn't quite sure what she wanted. Only that she wouldn't speak and end it.

Strange, but his gaze felt hot where it touched her skin. The night was warm but she shivered, anyway, and he moved, pushing her down on the bed before his hands slid down to cover her breasts.

They were too small, but he didn't seem to mind. His touch was feather soft, arousing, frustrating, and then he leaned forward and put his open mouth against hers, kissing her.

She held very still, trying to be calm as he kissed her, but when he pushed his tongue into her mouth she jumped, panicked, trying to scoot away from him.

He didn't let her, catching her shoulders and hauling her back. "That's nothing, Libby," he said. "You may as well relax and get used to it. My mouth, my tongue, my fingers. I'm going to touch you, taste you, everywhere, until you don't know where you end and I begin. And all you have to do, love—'' he brushed his lips against hers ''—is say no.''

She held her breath, and he put his mouth against hers again, lingering for a long, tantalizing moment. ''Just say no,'' he whispered in his harsh, strained voice. He covered her mouth, using his tongue again, and this time she didn't jump. ''Oh, God, please don't say no,'' he whispered.

She lifted her clenched hands off the mattress beside her and slid them around his neck. And she kissed him back, badly, she knew, but it didn't matter. Anger had vanished, shame and wisdom and second thoughts. He'd promised to show her, and she was going to take him up on that promise. She needed to know what it was like.

But first he showed her how to kiss. He caught her face in his hands and kissed her, slowly, deliberately, toying with her, calming her, arousing her, using his lips and his tongue and his teeth, coaxing her into doing the same, until she was suddenly breathless, panting, not with fear but with the first raw tendrils of desire.

''That's good, Libby,'' he murmured, letting his lips trail down the side of her neck. ''There's nothing to be frightened of. And there's no hurry. No one's going to interrupt us—we've got all night, and I intend to take my time with you. I think you need to come twice…maybe three times before I do. To make up for lost time.'' He licked her nipple, and she fought back a little squeak.

He looked up at her through his long, tousled hair and grinned. ''You can make noises, you know. You can moan and shriek without using words, and they won't count, I promise you. Go ahead, Libby. Let me hear you moan.''

She wouldn't have, of course, except that he'd covered her breast with his mouth, sucking on her, and it seemed to strike a nerve that went straight down between her legs, and there was nothing she could do but make a strangled noise of sheer pleasure.

''That's a start,'' he said, blowing on her nipple where it was wet from his mouth. Her breath caught in her throat, and she found she was clutching the bed again, grabbing the sheet in her fists. ''You have perfect breasts. Not too big, not too small. Absolutely perfect.'' He put his mouth on her other breast, while his fingers toyed with the first, and she bit her lip, afraid she might cry out when she felt the faint, incredibly arousing touch of his teeth against her.

Just when she thought she couldn't stand it anymore he moved his mouth away, down her belly, tasting, biting, nibbling at her skin. She was too dazed to realize that at some point he'd unfastened her shorts, and by the time she knew what he was doing he'd pulled them off her legs and thrown them on the floor. "That's better," he murmured. "I was getting impatient. Let's get the first one out of the way." And he put his mouth between her legs.

She felt a moment of grim satisfaction. If he thought that would work he was going to be surprised. Other men had tried it, and it had left her entirely unmoved. It had seemed to excite Richard, though, so she'd let him do it, but if John thought it was going to have any effect on her...

She caught her breath as an odd shiver danced across her skin. What had she been thinking about? Oh, yes, that it wouldn't have any effect on her...

Another shiver, this one harder, longer, and she realized she might possibly have been mistaken. She unfastened her death grip on the sheets and tried to push him away, but he simply caught her hands in his so she couldn't interfere.

It was like a slow fire licking at her, a strange sort of tickle that made her crazy, and she jerked, trying to move him, but he ignored her, concentrating on the task at hand, and she opened her mouth to tell him to stop when her body convulsed in a sharp, deep spasm, so intense it was almost painful. She fought it, panicked, and he slid up beside her.

"You did it again," he said. "What are you afraid of?"

She was trembling, her body feeling almost

cramped from the small explosion that had raced through her. She wanted this done and over with—it was too disturbing, too upsetting, too impossible.

He kissed her mouth, and he tasted like sex. "We'll count that one, but just barely," he said. "Let's try something else."

Enough was enough. She tried to scramble off the bed, not quite certain her legs would hold her, but he simply hauled her back, against him, her back up against his stomach, his arms holding her tight. She remembered waking that way in the rain forest. It seemed centuries ago, and yet it had only been yesterday. But there was no safety in his arms now, only demand and danger, as he wrapped an imprisoning arm around her waist, pulling her tight against him, and put his other hand between her legs.

"I know, you hate this," he mocked in a gentle whisper. "I'm doing terrible things to you and you can't make me stop, and all you want is for me to go away and leave you alone. Is that it?"

How did he know just how to touch her, just where? She squirmed in his arms, but it only felt better, and she knew that this time she wouldn't be able to stop, wouldn't be able to control it, and she wasn't sure why she even wanted to.

"That's right, love," he whispered against her ear. "That's better. Move against me. Show me

what you like. Do you like it hard? Or softer? Or
a little bit of both? I'm here to please.''

She was shaking and she couldn't stop. Everything he did to her was one more frustration, one
more delight. When he licked her ear she wanted
to howl. When he bit her shoulder she climaxed,
and this time she couldn't stop it. It rocked her
body, and she heard her voice cry out, a thin, high-
pitched wail, as her body shook and twisted in dark,
unthinkable pleasure.

She could barely breathe when he turned her on
her back and covered her, sliding deep inside her,
so deep she choked. She wanted to beg him to stop,
to give her time. She needed to find her defenses,
to find safety somewhere, but there was no safety
with him in her body, surging, pushing deeper, faster. He caught her legs and pulled them around his
hips, and unbelievably she wanted more, she
wanted all of him. She clutched his shoulders, her
fingers digging in tight, and his answering growl
was one of animal pleasure, and she knew that this
time she wouldn't be able to climax, not this way,
not at all, not again.

They were both slippery with sweat in the night
air, sliding against each other, and she could barely
hold on to him. She let out a soft, despairing cry,
afraid he was slipping away from her as she felt the
ice begin to freeze her once more, when he muttered, ''No you don't, love. Not this time.'' And he

reached between their bodies and touched her, hard, just as he filled her so deeply he pushed her halfway across the bed.

She screamed, but it didn't stop, it just went on, endlessly, rolling over and over in the darkness, wave upon wave of hot, prickly sensation that threatened to shatter her. She felt him go rigid in her arms, the sweet flow between them, and she knew she was crying again, those damned tears.

She was still shaking, racked by stray spasms, when he withdrew from her and pulled her into his arms. She buried her face against his chest, hiding, weeping, as he held her. He kissed the top of her head, her cheekbones, every place he could reach.

And finally, when she'd stopped crying, when she could breathe again, when she could move without another orgasm shimmering through her, she lifted her head and looked into his eyes.

''Yes,'' she said.

Chapter Fourteen

The night was endless, over in moments. He pulled the mosquito netting around them, closing them in a curtained wonderland, closing out the world. And she talked to him. She told him of silly things, of things that mattered. And he talked to her. Things he said he'd never told anyone else, and she believed him. And they made love. Endlessly. He took her body beyond limits she hadn't even realized existed, and he coaxed her past fear and shyness until, by morning, she was a glorious, brazen vixen. He pulled her onto his lap, letting her find him, fill herself with him, and he sat back, not moving, under iron control, while she learned what pleasured her, how to bring herself to the very edge and then hold back, just slightly, to make it more powerful. And he lay back against the pillows, watching her out of half-closed eyes, and this time it was his fists that clutched the sheets until they ripped in his hands, while she moved against him, taking him deep inside her.

She could feel the heated tingles dancing against her skin, feel the shuttered darkness begin to close in, and she slowed, clutching his shoulders, pleading. "Finish it," she gasped. "I can't..."

He shook his head, but she could feel the fierce tension running through his body, and she knew the price it cost him to deny her. "You do it," he said. "You tell me when."

"I can't," she said, but she began to move again, unable to stop herself, needing more of him, needing all of him, needing what he was holding back, and when she felt herself begin to fly apart she cried out.

"Now!" she gasped, and he was with her, immediately, joining with her as they tumbled into oblivion.

She collapsed against him, breathless, sweating, and she kissed his mouth, laughing. He reached up to cup her face, holding her still, when there was a sudden noisy pounding at the front door.

They both froze. Libby tried to pull away from him, but he caught her and held her, still inside her. "Who is it?" he called out, sounding about as welcoming as a wild boar.

"Who the hell do you think it is, mate?" A voice called back. "It's your old pal Roger, here to pick up a young lady and deliver her to the mainland. Unless you've changed your mind.''

Dead silence. He tilted his head back and looked up at her. "No," he said finally. "I haven't changed my mind. Give us a half an hour and I'll bring her down to the dock.''

"Make it fifteen minutes. I've got a schedule to keep.''

John didn't try to stop her as she pulled free, sliding off the bed. "I'll be ready in ten," she said, grabbing her discarded clothes and heading for the door.

"Libby…''

She turned to look at him. "Yes?''

She didn't know what she expected him to say. To beg her to stay? Not likely.

She hadn't even realized how light it was. It must be midmorning. The candles had guttered out sometime during the night, and the mosquito netting lay tangled around the bed. She couldn't even remember when they tore it down, though she had vague memories of the two of them being tangled in it.

"Nothing," he said.

She stood there with her clothes held to her naked body, looking at him. He'd done exactly what he said he was going to do and no more. He'd given her the best night of sex she could even begin to imagine. He hadn't offered anything else.

She turned to go, thanking God that she'd wept

enough during the night, only to step in something soft and gooey. She looked down to see that she'd stepped in her discarded pan of brownies. Right at a time when she really needed chocolate.

She took the fastest shower on record, threw on the clothes she'd brought with her, shoved her feet in her battered sandals and started out the door to the dock, hoping against hope that she'd get out of there without seeing John again. She was halfway to the small, compact steamboat when she realized he was standing there talking to the captain, wearing nothing but a pair of shorts. And that her shirt smelled like him.

She looked down. There was a spaghetti stain on the front, and she hadn't had spaghetti last night. She'd accidentally taken his shirt from the floor, and there was nothing she could do about it at this point, short of ripping it off and going topless to the mainland.

She could handle it, she told herself. She'd faced worse things and survived. How much worse could it get?

John had his back turned to her, deep in conversation with the weather-beaten, sandy-haired man who seemed to be the entire crew of the disreputable-looking steamer. John had a bite mark on the side of his neck. Scratches on his back. A love bruise right above his hip. She could only imagine what else was covered up.

Miraculously she didn't blush. After last night she was past blushing. "There's the little lady now," the captain said. "Now, don't you worry, miss, old Roger will see to everything. There are not many people John Hunter trusts, but I'm proud to say I'm one of them. I'll see you safely on your way back to your people."

She smiled at him, studiously ignoring John as she climbed aboard the boat. "You're very kind."

Roger gave her a gold-toothed grin. "Always glad to help a damsel in distress, I am. Though I think John's a damned fool—"

"Thanks, Roger." John interrupted him calmly, forestalling his comments. "I'll see you when you get back. Libby…?" He turned to her, but she'd moved carefully out of his way. She had no idea how he planned to say goodbye to her, but she wasn't taking any chances. If he touched her, kissed her, she'd probably throw herself at his feet and beg him not to send her away. And that would be excruciatingly horrible for both of them.

So she scurried behind Roger, out of reach, and gave him a bright, cheery smile. It didn't reach her eyes, but John was, after all, a man. He'd believe what he wanted to believe, and not look for hidden meanings.

"Thanks for everything, John," she said breezily. "I'll send you a postcard when I get back to Chicago."

He stared at her, an odd, arrested expression on his face, and for a long, breathless moment she thought he would do just what she wanted. Take her by the hand and drag her off the boat, back to the house. He'd kidnapped her twice already—why couldn't he make it a nice round number like three?

"Goodbye, Libby," he said. And he turned and jumped off the boat, walking back up the wooden walkway to the house. A moment later he'd disappeared inside, without looking back even once.

"Well, I'd say he's a right fool," Roger said, untying the boat. The engine was already running, and it took him less than a moment to steer the craft into the water. "But then, I expect you know that, don't you, miss? Sun's pretty bright out here, ain't it? Don't blame you for squinting." He gave her a sympathetic smile. "Why don't you go below and get yourself a nice cuppa while I make some distance between us and that miserable old hermit. Nothing grieves me more than a man who doesn't appreciate what he's got."

She tried her absolute best to manage a breezy smile, but it fell far short, and Captain Roger knew the difference. "Go below, miss, and take a little nap. You'll feel better once we hit the mainland."

"How...long will it take?" It was only a slight hiccup, and he couldn't have known she was trying desperately not to cry. Or at least, he couldn't be certain.

"Three or four hours, depending on the tides," said Captain Roger. "No time at all, miss. You'll be there in time for a late lunch. A little food and a cold beer always makes things look better. As a matter of fact, there's a cold beer or two below if you're feeling the need."

She shook her head. "No, thanks. But I—" hiccup "—think I will lie down for a while."

"You do that, miss. I'll call you when we get near land."

She disappeared down the companionway, and Roger shook his head. Most people were damned fools, but he'd always figured John Hunter had more brains than most. Guess he was mistaken, and he had every intention of telling him so once he got back.

And maybe it wouldn't be too late for that sweet little thing sobbing her heart out down in the cabin.

JOHN WALKED STRAIGHT through the house and onto the porch that ran along the back of it. He didn't hesitate, diving into the forest that surrounded his place with a single-minded determination. He broke into a run, covering the ground swiftly, barely aware of his surroundings. It wasn't until he'd reached the top of the cliffs that he realized what he'd been doing. He'd been running away from Libby.

Because if he'd stayed back at the house, stood

on the porch and watched her leave, he wouldn't have let her go. And that would have been crazy for both of them.

He could see the little steamer moving down the coast, and there was Roger at the helm, probably singing some bawdy song like he always did, John thought. Or maybe not, out of deference to his passenger.

There was no sign of Libby, and he cursed beneath his breath. If he'd any idea that this hilltop had been his eventual destination he would have stopped and grabbed some binoculars.

She must be in the cabin taking a nap. It would be little wonder—she'd had a very energetic night with only a few catnaps.

Catnaps. She'd curled up against him, practically purring, and a wave of longing that was only half-sexual and entirely emotional washed over him. He wanted her back. He wanted her sleeping with him, whispering with him, loving with him.

And he was being a damned fool. He wasn't made for cohabiting, and she wasn't made for the wilderness. They were completely mismatched, and it was far better to end it after a great night of sex.

The best sex of her life, he'd promised her. But the damnable thing was, it had been the best sex of his life as well, and he'd had a lot more to compare it to.

He watched until the boat steamed out of sight,

hoping irrationally for one last glimpse of her. But there was no one on the deck but Roger, and eventually it was no more than a tiny speck in the distance. And then it was gone.

He was half tempted to just keep walking, straight into the forest, but he controlled the need. Instead he headed back down to the cottage, at a much slower pace, in no hurry to go back.

It was just as he'd left it. The first thing he had to do was clean up. She was gone, and it wouldn't do any good to have reminders all over the place.

He started with the bedroom. The sheet was ripped and stained, and he supposed he ought to just toss it in the trash. Instead he put it in the hamper. He grabbed the mosquito netting and wrapped it into a ball, tossing it in the closet, trying not to remember what they'd been doing when she'd pulled it down around them.

This was going to be fine, he told himself. No problem. He wasn't even missing her, just a little leftover sexual angst, but that would pass, and he could settle in and get back to his research....

And that's when he saw the brownie pan on the floor, with her footprint as clear as day. He picked it up, staring down at it as if it were some miraculous prehistoric artifact. And for some damned fool reason he set it on the kitchen counter rather than tossing it.

He was sitting on the lanai, on his second beer

and feeling about as cheerful as a martyr on the way to the stake, when he heard the sounds of the steamer on its return trip, and he felt a sudden stirring in the pit of his stomach. What if she'd flat-out refused to leave? What if she told Roger she was coming back, and he couldn't stop her?

Not that Roger would stop her. He thought John was a damned fool for letting her go, and he would have happily carted her all the way back. Roger was a sentimental old fool. He still believed in true love and all that garbage.

What would he do if she came back? He'd have to make certain things clear, of course. There'd have to be ground rules—he wasn't used to living with anyone else, and she wasn't the type to just fade into the woodwork. She was even more obtrusive when she was being silent.

But he could manage to put up with it, quite nicely, as a matter of fact. She hadn't said anything about wanting to stay, but he'd only had to take one look at her face from across the boat to know that she would. If he'd only asked.

Roger was right, he was a damned fool sometimes. But Roger didn't know Libby. She may have let him send her away, but sooner or later on that five-hour trip her temper was going to get the better of her, and he'd be willing to bet anything that she was coming back to him, right this minute, ready to give him a piece of her mind. He just had to talk her into giving him a piece of her heart.

She wasn't on the deck as Roger pulled up to the dock, but he didn't let that discourage him. She was probably still below, trying to figure out her best plan of attack.

Except that Roger didn't look particularly happy as he tied up the boat and hopped out. Not happy with life in general, and not happy with John in particular.

"You got another one of those beers, mate?" he called out. "I've had one hell of a day."

"I've been saving this one for you," he said, handing him one. Still no sign of life at the boat. How was she going to handle this?

"What the hell are you looking at?" Roger demanded irritably. "You think the *Katie O.* is going to sink?"

He turned to look at Roger. "Are you alone?"

"Of course I'm alone, you great stupid fool! You think she'd come back after you kicked her out and didn't even kiss her goodbye? She spent the whole damned trip down in the cabin crying her heart out. You're one right bastard, you know that."

John took a long drink of his beer, ignoring the chill, sick feeling that hit his stomach. "Yeah, I know," he said evenly.

"Lucky for you she found some old friends of hers. I wouldn't have wanted to leave her alone in town, but she met up with a couple of blokes and went off with them, arm in arm...."

"She did what?"

"No need to get your knickers in a twist!" Roger said. "You let her go, you know. Besides, they weren't anything more than friends. One big, ugly guy and a little weaselly fellow. Can't imagine where she knew them from, but they were as thick as thieves, rushing her out of there before I could even say goodbye."

"Hell and damnation," said John. "Give me ten minutes."

"Ten minutes for what, mate?"

"We're going after her." He was already heading for the front door.

"I'm not making a special trip all the way back to Johnson Harbour because you happened to screw up your love life. You'll just have to wait—"

"I can't wait. Those weren't her friends, Roger. They'll kill her."

Roger stared at him blankly. "Well, what are you waiting for then? Let's get the hell back there."

"Now, ain't this convenient?" Alf said jovially as they hurried her along the narrow streets of Johnson Harbour. "Here we were, ready to hire a boat to go checking some of the outer islands for any trace of you, and you walk straight into our arms. Must be bloody fate, don't you think, Mick?"

"Must be," Mick mumbled.

"And don't think of making a noise, missy. I can break your neck so quickly no one will even notice, and we'll tell people you've got sunstroke. You're not ready to die yet, are you?"

"No," Libby mumbled.

"Then you'll do as I say. There's the car up ahead. You climb in the back seat, all nice and ladylike, and don't make a peep, or Mick will have to hurt you."

She turned to look at Mick. He had an utterly miserable expression on his face, but she didn't for one moment doubt that he'd do what Alf told him to do.

The car was an anonymous rental. Alf was taking no chances—he blocked the door as he helped her in, so she had no chance of escape. Mick had climbed in the other side, and she was well and truly trapped.

She had two seconds to plead while Alf walked around to the driver's seat. "Mick, you don't want to do this," she said urgently. "You don't want to hurt me, you know you don't."

"No, miss," he said miserably. "And I promise you, I won't. I'll make sure Alf does it neat and tidy. No pain at all. Trust me."

It didn't warm the cockles of her heart. Alf got in the driver's seat and the car sagged. He glanced at Libby in the rearview mirror, and she glared at him, resisting the childish impulse to stick her tongue out at him. For some reason the idea of sticking her tongue out at her future murderer seemed a bit...ludicrous.

"Looks like our little lady's been having herself some fun while she's been gone," Alf observed. "Doesn't she have the look of someone who's been royally shagged? Where is he, Doc?"

"Go to hell," she said sweetly.

"I tried to be reasonable," Alf said with a sigh. "You can tell Old Ed that, if he asks. Give her the shot, Mick. We want her nice and peaceful while we bring her back to Ghost Island."

"No!" Libby cried, but Mick had already jabbed her arm with a syringe. She recognized those syringes—they were the ones she'd emptied and filled with water, dumping out the potent tranquilizers. It was a perfect chance. All she had to do was fake it and they'd stop watching her, and she'd be able to escape, and...

She could feel her hands and feet growing numb, and she realized with horror that, by sheer luck, they'd gotten one of the syringes she hadn't sabotaged.

"Hell and damnation," she muttered thickly as the darkness closed in around her.

Chapter Fifteen

There was one good thing to be said for being kid-napped and drugged, Libby thought some un-counted hours later. If the drugs were strong enough, she didn't have to suffer through that god-awful plane ride in a conscious state. By the time things started coming back into focus she was al-ready back on Ghost Island, traveling along in the back seat of the same luxurious limo that had brought her there a lifetime ago.

She let out a small, involuntary moan. "Awake, are you?" Alf said with demonic cheer. "We timed that just about right, didn't we? Softhearted Mick here was afraid it might have been too big a dose, given that it was calibrated for your ape-man friend, but I figured even though you were small you had a lot of fight in you. And here you are, wide awake, right on cue."

She glared at him, leaning back against the elegant leather seats, this time having no illusions about the luxury. It might as well be an executioner's cart.

How long had it been since she arrived here? A lifetime ago, when she'd been an entirely different woman. If she'd known what was going to happen, would she have changed her mind? If she had the chance, would she go back to being the edgy, nervous creature that she had been?

If she got out of this alive she was going to have that chance. She'd go back to her old life, her old city, and maybe she'd turn back into the old Libby. She devoutly hoped not.

But it was more than likely she wasn't going anywhere at all. Alf didn't have a speck of conscience, and Mick, though regretful, did his bidding. As for Hunnicutt, he gave the orders and then washed his hands of the matter.

The one thing she wasn't going to do was tell them a damned thing about John. About who he was, or where to find him. It wouldn't make any difference in what they did to her, and the least she could do was try to protect him.

Not that he deserved protecting after letting her walk out like that this morning, but it seemed a waste of time to hold a grudge when she was staring death in the face. Might as well die being noble.

Alf pulled up in front of the long, low building,

and Libby reached for the door, planning one last attempt at escaping. It didn't open.

"Now, you didn't think it was going to be that easy, did you?" Alf chided her. "Even the most luxurious cars come with child safety locks. You just stay right there and Mick will come around and escort you into the house. There are dangerous creatures in the jungle out there. We wouldn't want you to run into any wild animals, now, would we?"

If she'd thought Mick was having second thoughts, his grip on her arm disabused her of the notion. There would be no escaping his grip, even if she could manage to distract him for a moment. She let them lead her up the front steps, feeling tired, grubby and still slightly looped. She had to admit that as far as knockout drugs went, this was far more enjoyable than the tranquilizer dart.

Once inside the cool, dark hallway the door closed behind them, and subtle lighting illuminated their way. She started toward the living room, where she'd first met Hunnicutt, when Alf caught her arm in his meaty grip. "Not that way, girlie. He's waiting for us in the library."

He propelled her down to the other end of the hallway, into a wide, spacious, brightly lit room. The walls were covered with bookshelves, and the books were color-coordinated, arranged by size, and had obviously never been read. In the middle was a huge wooden desk, with Edward J. Hunnicutt sitting there waiting for her.

"Hi, Ed," she said with cheerful defiance. "Long time no see."

Hunnicutt raised his eyebrows in surprise, throwing a questioning look at Alf. "You sound surprisingly cheerful, Dr. Holden, given the circumstances."

"Oh, I'm a firm believer in the saying that if life gives you lemons, make lemonade. Mind if I sit down?"

"Please." He gestured toward one of the leather chairs. "I must say you look very different from when I first saw you five days ago. I'm very disappointed in your behavior. Most unprofessional."

"Five days ago?" Libby echoed, fastening on what interested her. She realized with some amusement that she was, for want of a better word, slightly stoned from the drug they'd fed her. Just cheerfully feeling no pain, even as she stared death in the face. "My, my, how time flies when you're having fun."

"Do you have any explanation for your behavior, Dr. Holden?" Hunnicutt said severely. He reminded her of her high school principal, the one who'd fought long and hard against a fourteen-year-old graduating. She'd won, and he'd hated it.

This time she wasn't winning, but Old Ed wasn't happy about it, either. "Explanation?" she said vaguely. "Well, let's see. Compassion? Decency? Honor? Justice? This is a big library—I'm sure you could look those words up since you obviously don't know the meaning of them."

He was an ugly little man, despite his perfect hair and skin, his spotless suit, his bland features. Ugly in his soul, and it showed in his furious, colorless eyes.

"Where is the wild man, Dr. Holden?"

"Wild man? I don't know what you're talking about," she said, leaning back and crossing her long, bare legs.

"What other kind of drugs do you have downstairs in that laboratory, Mr. Droggan?" Hunnicutt asked, his calm voice belying his fury. "Dr. McDonough liked to play with pharmaceuticals—did he happen to leave some sodium pentathol or something of that ilk?"

"I don't think so, Mr. Hunnicutt. Just the tranquilizers, and most of those are broken. We've got a few syringes left for emergencies."

"We're not going to need them unless you can manage to find our subject and recapture him," Hunnicutt said. "And we'll have an easier time doing that if Dr. Holden would just be reasonable and tell us where he is."

Libby shrugged. "I haven't the faintest idea."

"Oh, we know that's not true. And I imagine Alf won't have too difficult a time getting information from you. Drugs are much more civilized, but if I know Mr. Droggan he probably prefers the old-fashioned way.''

"You promised you weren't going to hurt her," Mick piped up.

"If she'd cooperate there'd be no need to hurt her, Mr. Brown," said Hunnicutt, the soul of reason. "Maybe you should explain the situation to her."

"Maybe you should all go to hell," Libby said.

Hunnicutt shrugged. "You see? She leaves us no choice. I'm sure Alf will be moderately restrained, but you can never..." A sudden sharp beeping noise filled the room, and his colorless face turned even paler.

"I'll go see who it is," Alf said.

"How could someone have gotten on the island without anyone knowing?" Hunnicutt demanded in a peevish voice. "The security system here is unimpeachable."

"Probably the same way they got off the island," Alf said. "Don't worry, I'll get rid of whoever it is."

"Don't arouse their suspicions. You're not the most politic of people, Mr. Droggan. Be polite."

"What about her?" Alf jerked his head in Libby's direction.

"Give her another shot and hide her someplace. We can deal with her later."

"No!" Libby shrieked, but it was already too late. Mick had plunged another syringe into her arm with bloodthirsty enthusiasm, and she closed her eyes, waiting for the curtain of numbness to wash over her, trying to fight it, knowing it was a lost cause, knowing...

It wasn't working. This time they'd used one of the dud syringes, and all she had in her system was water. She let herself go limp, falling back against the chair in a sprawled-out, ungainly position.

"Is it supposed to work that fast?" Hunnicutt said doubtfully.

"Must have hit a vein. Besides, she was already loaded with the stuff. It wouldn't take much to put her under. What do you want me to do with her?"

"Answer the door. Mick can find some place to stash her."

"Well, don't take her too far, Mick, me lad. I've got some unfinished business with her."

It was hard enough trying to stay utterly limp when no one was touching her. Once Mick put his hands under her arms it took all her self-control not to start giggling. She'd always been hellaciously ticklish. He dragged her out of the chair, bumping her along the floor, and she concentrated on every boneless, soggy vision she could think of, from bread dough to wet washcloths to orange Jell-O. If he'd tried to drag her from the room she would have had to struggle, but as it was he just hauled her behind the sofa and dumped her.

"You're certain that's good enough?" Hunnicutt asked sharply.

"'Course it is," Mick replied. "They won't be looking behind your furniture, not without a search warrant, and she's got enough stuff in her to keep her out for a week."

"I don't want her out for a week. I want answers."

"Well, Alf'll see to that," Mick said cheerily. "Want I should go see what's keeping him?"

"Please," said Hunnicutt in a long-suffering voice.

The silence in the room was almost deafening. Libby lay perfectly still, even though her wrist was trapped under her body and her legs were at an uncomfortable angle. She could hardly shift without Hunnicutt noticing. Instead she'd simply bide her time. Sooner or later they'd leave her alone, and she could run for it. Unless, of course, whoever had broached his private kingdom had come to save her.

But who would even know she was there? For that matter, who would care? Not that stupid man on his stupid island who'd let her walk away without a word...

"Police," Alf said as the door slid open. "I couldn't stop 'em."

There was enough noise in the room now that

Libby could roll over without being heard. She scooted forward so that she could get a glimpse of what was going on. It looked like a whole army of police, legs and boots and someone in a dark suit and expensive shoes. She slid down further, trying to get a better look.''

"What can I do for you, gentlemen?" Edward J. Hunnicutt's mellow tones would have fooled most anyone, and Libby held her breath.

"I'm Detective Major Larrabbee of the Johnson Harbour Police, Mr. Hunnicutt. First off, we have a warrant for the arrest of Alfred Droggan, also known as Orville Johnson and for Michael Brown, also known as Mick the Ferret, for the murder of Dr. William McDonough and the abduction of Dr. Elizabeth Holden. There's also a question of charges against you, sir, for unlawful restraint, environmental crimes, trafficking in controlled substances—"

"Don't be absurd!" Hunnicutt protested, shocked. "My environmental record is spotless! As for drugs, I have no interest or need to be involved in illegal drugs...."

"Experimental tranquilizers for both humans and animals, Mr. Hunnicutt. They're only illegal if you don't hold a doctor's degree, and as far as I know, the three of you don't."

"I think this conversation is at an end," Hunnicutt said pleasantly. "You can talk to my legal department."

"Where is she?" It was a new voice, one she didn't recognize for a moment. Australian, slightly raspy. And then she knew.

"I have no idea who you're talking about," Hunnicutt said stiffly. There was a pause. "Have we met? You look vaguely familiar."

"No," said John calmly. "We've never met."

"You're not going to let them take us, are you, boss?" Alf demanded hoarsely. "You promised us you'd look out for us."

"Don't worry, Mr. Droggan, my lawyers will have this all cleared up in no time and the two of you will be released. I have no idea what they're talking about. Dr. McDonough died in a car accident, and Dr. Holden left my employ voluntarily several days ago. I'm afraid I have no idea where she is."

That was a cue if ever she heard one. Libby put her hands on the back of the sofa and hauled herself up. She was still feeling weak and shaky from the drugs, but her mood had improved enormously.

"Oops," she said. "I must have slipped your mind."

"Damn it!" Alf screeched. "What the hell did you do, Mick? I told you to give her the full syringe. She should be out like a light!"

"I did what you told me, Alf, I swear," Mick

said tearfully. "I don't know what's wrong with her...."

But Libby wasn't particularly interested in Mick's pleas. Instead she was looking at the one man who stood off to one side, in a dark suit, definitely Italian, probably Armani, though why the hell he should have an Armani suit was beyond her. He looked elegant, civilized, like a stranger.

But it didn't matter. He'd come for her.

"I don't know who this woman is or what she's doing here, but..."

"If I were you, Hunnicutt, I'd wait for your lawyers," John said calmly. He reached behind the sofa and hauled her over it, effortlessly, into his arms.

Alf and Mick were already in handcuffs, arguing. "He'll get away with it," Alf was fuming. "That's what always happens. The workers get it in the arse and the bosses go free."

"Don't you worry about it, Alfie," Mick said soothingly. "We haven't been in the slammer for years—it'll seem like old times. And when we get out, let's go into business for ourselves this time. It's no fun being a minion. We need to be independent contractors. Look on it like a vacation, old boy. Three squares a day, nice climate, no women around to make demands. The days will go by in a flash, you mark my words."

"More likely the years," said the man who appeared to be the senior officer. "Come along then.

And Mr. Hunnicutt, I would suggest you not leave here until we've had a chance to sit down with you and your lawyers. There are some very serious charges being made, and we intend to get to the bottom of them.''

Alf paused at the door, turning to stare at John. "Don't I know you?" he demanded suspiciously.

"I don't think so," he replied, keeping a protective arm around Libby. "How's your arm?"

A look of dawning realization swept over Alf's beefy face, followed by complete horror. Before he could do more than sputter, he was gone, with Mick still chattering cheerfully about the lovely time they'd have in jail.

Libby was leaning against John in a cheerfully bemused state. The detective came over to them. "You'd best take your lady out of here, Mr. Hunter," he said kindly. "She looks done in. We can take it from here."

"Thanks, Reg," he said. "Come along, Libby. We'll find you a nice place to sleep it off."

"I already slept it off," she said, dignified in her shorts and sandals and complete lack of underwear. "And I'm not sure I want to go anywhere with you. You don't love me."

He looked absolutely appalled. Hunnicutt cleared his throat, and even the police detective looked as if his collar was too tight.

But John rallied, braver than she'd expected.

"What makes you say that?" he asked in a calm, conversational voice, taking her arm in his and leading her out into the hall, away from their curious witnesses.

"You let me go. You didn't try to stop me."

"You didn't want to stay."

"You didn't ask me."

"Okay," he said. "I'm asking you."

She blinked. "Asking me what?"

"Asking you to stay."

She'd lost the gist of the conversation completely. "Stay where?"

He patted her arm soothingly. "With me, Libby. Back on the island. Come along."

"But you don't love me," she said plaintively, harking back to her original argument with bulldoglike tenacity.

"Of course I do. Let's go home."

She narrowed her gaze suspiciously. "Do I have to fly?"

"Darling, you're already flying," he said sweetly.

"Because if you make me get in another one of those tiny airplanes I'm not sure that you're worth it."

"I'm worth it," he said confidently. "And I promise to distract you on the plane."

She looked doubtful. "How?"

"Leave it to me. I'm very inventive."

She was tired of arguing, so she simply leaned her head on his shoulder and let him lead her out of that spotless, soulless bunker. The evening air was warm and humid, and Libby didn't wake up until they'd landed safely in Johnson Harbour.

It was almost midnight, and Captain Roger was waiting for them. "You see what kind of trouble you could have saved yourself if you'd just shown a little sense in the first place?" Roger said. "You take that poor little thing down below and get her something to eat. She looks worn-out."

She gave Roger a wan smile. "I'm not hungry."

"Then you let her rest. If I were twenty years younger she wouldn't have to settle for a sorry specimen like you," he grumbled. "But I'm warning you now, you treat her right or you'll have me to answer to."

"Yes, sir," John said with surprising seriousness. "I will."

And Captain Roger turned to the tiller and began to sing a cheerfully bawdy song at the top of his lungs.

Chapter Sixteen

Captain Roger had lit an oil lamp in the tiny cabin, illuminating its cozy reaches. The bed where she'd lain and wept that morning was over in the corner, still unmade, and she went and climbed on it, sitting cross-legged as she turned to look at John. It was the first time they'd been alone since he'd brought her out of Hunnicutt's fortress, and she suddenly felt shy.

"What are we going to do now?" she asked.

He appeared to consider the question far more seriously than it deserved. "I've had a lot of time to think about it, and I've come up with some alternative. Number one, I could come back to Chicago with you."

"But I—"

"Let me finish. I hate cities, I hate the cold, but if I had to, I'd do it. I just don't want to. The second alternative is that you come back to the island with me. The problem is, you like cities, you like civilization, and you like people.''

"I'm not sure if that's true after this week," she said caustically.

"All right, let's say you like people more than I do," he qualified. "You also like it here more than I like it in the States. However, it still wouldn't be fair to ask you to give up everything and stay here."

"But I didn't—"

"There's a third alternative," he continued, riding roughshod over her protests. A habit he was going to have to learn to break, she thought fondly. "We live on the island. You have to understand that every now and then even that much civilization is too much for me, and I have to get away. The Australians call it a walkabout. I just need to disappear into the bush for weeks and sometimes even months until I get my bearings back. When that happens, you could go back and spend time in the city. Actually, you could go back any time you wanted, but this way, it would work out best for both of us."

"You *have* been putting a lot of thought into this, haven't you?" She didn't let her voice give away a thing.

"Have you come up with any alternatives? If you're worried about the cost of flying back and forth to the States, I wouldn't if I were you. For one thing, I have pretty much more money than I can ever use in a lifetime. And I'm willing to bet that Hunnicutt decides granting you a generous severance package is the proper thing to do.''

"That's all he has to do?"

"I'm expecting he'll deed Ghost Island and the research facility to the University of Cairns and promise never to set foot in Australia again. Of course they won't hold him to it—he's got deep-enough pockets that he'll be welcomed with open arms in a couple of years. Maybe by then he'll have developed a new hobby. So what do you think?"

"Fine," she said.

"Fine?" he echoed. "That's all you have to say?"

"Fine, I'll come back to the island with you, fine that I'll stay with you until you decide you need to wander off, and that's when I'll get my fix of civilization. It sounds very practical. But actually that wasn't what I was asking you."

"It wasn't?"

"No," she said. "I mean, what are we going to do *now?*"

His surprise was only temporary. He glanced back at the door. "There's a lock. Not that Roger ever comes below when he's piloting the *Katie O*. The engines make a hell of a noise—covers up almost anything. Though he said he could hear you crying on the way to Johnson Harbour."

"He was lying," she said flatly, daring him to contradict her. "Then we've got four hours to kill. Why don't you start by taking off that damned suit?"

His grin was slow, seductive. "You mean you don't like my Armani?"

"Why in heaven's name would you need Armani?"

"I teach classes every now and then."

"No one teaches in Armani, trust me on this. Lose the tie."

He unknotted it, slowly, his long, dark fingers working the knot loose. He pulled it free from the collar and draped it around her shoulders, then stepped back to look at it speculatively. "You know, there are some entertaining things we can do with that tie...."

"Not now. Take off the coat."

"Yes, ma'am." He stripped off the jacket, laying it across a chair.

"Now the shoes."

"These are specially made Italian leather. I've spent so many years of my life barefoot that I can't wear ready-made shoes."

"I like you barefoot," she said. "Take them off."

He kicked out of them, then peeled off his socks. "What about the shirt? Egyptian cotton?"

"It'll make nice dish towels. And don't start telling me you can think of entertaining uses for your leather belt. I have my limits.''

''Coward,'' he said, laughing. ''Do I get to keep my pants on?''

''Oh, most definitely not. Lose 'em, sailor.''

He unzipped them and shoved them down, kicking out of them.

''You're wearing boxers?'' she said in disbelief.

''Hey, I was in disguise,'' he protested.

''I don't think Hunnicutt and his goons were going to check your underwear.'' Her voice was caustic.

''You never can be too careful,'' he said, moving toward the bunk. ''I think I'm getting a little ahead of you. Why don't you get rid of that T-shirt?''

''Oh, damn!'' she said suddenly.

He knelt on the edge of the bunk. It was narrow, with barely room for two. ''What?''

''I forgot to get my clothes when we were at Ghost Island! I didn't even get anything at Johnson Harbour! I have nothing to wear when we get back to the island.''

''Somehow,'' John said, ''I don't think that will be a problem.'' And he pushed her down on the mattress, covering her body with his.

Captain Roger stopped singing long enough to take a healthy slug of beer. He'd been smart enough to bring a few up to keep him company for the trip back to the island—he knew perfectly well he wasn't going to see hide nor hair of John and his young lady for the duration. Already he could hear muffled laughter drifting up from the cabin.

"Looks like you're finally showing some sense, mate," he said, raising an invisible toast to the cabin.

And once more he began to sing.

Three months later

THEY'D HAD A FIGHT, and Libby was miserable. It wasn't their first fight—John had spent too much of his life alone, not taking anyone else's opinions into account, for it to be smooth sailing, but each time the battle raged they worked it out, first verbally, then physically.

But that wasn't possible this time. He was gone. No warning, no apology, no nothing. She'd slept in that morning, exhausted after an energetic night, only to find him in the kitchen, dressed in what she could only think of as his Wild Man clothes, and she knew he was leaving.

She had two possible reactions—tears or anger, and she decided to go with anger. She was already feeling far too vulnerable, and crying in front of him would only make it worse. So she'd taken refuge in sarcasm, he'd responded in same, and eventually he'd stormed out of the house without saying goodbye.

And then, even worse, he'd stormed back in, picked her up and kissed her so thoroughly she could still feel it days later, and then left again. All without a word.

That was when she'd cried. And then she became calm and practical. He'd return, he said he would, he always did, and this would give her time to go back to the city, to see the old places and the old friends. To shop, to visit museums, to be in the hustle and bustle of city life.

Which no longer interested her. Her friends had been Richard's friends, not really hers, and in the year since he'd dumped her she'd been too obsessed with work to make new ones. She could buy anything she wanted on the Internet, and the very thought of the hustle and bustle and noise and crowds filled her with horror. But she dutifully made her reservation, had Captain Roger pick her up, and got as far as Johnson Harbour.

This time it wasn't Mick and Alf who stopped her. And when she turned back to the *Katie O.*, Captain Roger simply grinned and held out a gnarled hand to help her back on board.

He'd been gone a week. A week alone in that big bed, a week of solitude and silence that wasn't half-bad once she got used to it. She'd grown to love the quiet noises the jungle made, the sound of the waves lapping on the shore, the cry of the night birds. It was a better place with John there, but even without him it was a better place than anywhere else.

But God, she missed him.

It was just past dawn when she woke up suddenly, jerked out of sleep by an unexpected noise. She sat up in bed, pulling the sheet up around her, her heart racing. She slept in one of John's oversize T-shirts and nothing else, and her robe was in the bathroom. She could hear someone moving around in the front room, making no effort to be stealthy. Whoever it was must have thought they were both gone.

John didn't even own a gun. He said he didn't believe in them, and neither did Libby, but right at that moment she was ready to convert. She slipped out of bed, yanking the sheet off after her and draping it around her as she tiptoed toward the door. She could always sneak out the back and hide. Whoever it was would have to leave sooner or later, and Captain Roger said he'd come by and check on her every couple of days.

She opened the bedroom door just a crack, listening. She could hear a voice, low-pitched, familiar, and relief swamped her. It was John. But who the hell could he be talking to? Had he brought someone back here?

She pushed open the bedroom door, ready to kill him if there was a woman in the living room. His back was toward the hallway, and she realized he was alone. Talking on the cell phone he'd acquired when she moved in.

She didn't move, just watched him as calm well-being flooded her body. She wasn't right without him. It didn't make sense, it was weak and ridiculous, but it was fact. She needed him to feel whole.

"I need to send a cable. It's for Dr. Elizabeth Holden, Drake Hotel, Chicago, Illinois. Yes, I'll hold." He ran a restless hand through his hair. It was tangled, his beard had started growing again, and he looked exhausted. "Yes, I'm ready. The text should read 'Come back to me.'"

"I never left," she said.

He spun around, staring at her as if he'd seen a ghost. And then he dropped the phone, crossed the room and picked her up in his arms. His grip was so strong it almost hurt, and he was trembling. "Don't," he whispered in her hair. "Don't leave me."

"Never," she said, holding him. "I love you."

The sun was coming up, blazing into the front windows of the small house, filling it with light and warmth. And there was nothing more to be said.

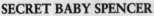
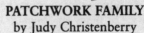

COMING NEXT MONTH

Visit us at www.eHarlequin.com

CNM1000